About the author

Connie Spanhake is the author of the mystery novel, *Finding Me*. Raised in a military family, she loves to travel, especially when it involves a beach. She loves reading, photography and gardening. When she is not researching for her next book, she enjoys spending time with her family in Upstate New York. To find out more, visit her website at conniespanhake.com.

DARK SECRETS

Connie Spanhake

DARK SECRETS

Vanguard Press

A CIP catalogue record for this title is
available from the British Library.

ISBN 978-1-80016-063-7

*Vanguard Press is an imprint of
Pegasus Elliot MacKenzie Publishers Ltd.*
www.pegasuspublishers.com

First Published in 2021

**Vanguard Press
Sheraton House Castle Park
Cambridge England**

Printed & Bound in Great Britain

Dedication

For my mother, the strongest woman I know.

Acknowledgements

I would like to acknowledge a few people without whom this book would not have been possible.

I would like to say a huge thank you to my husband, Roy Spanhake, for always supporting and encouraging me, and my parents who are always asking questions and keep me on track. I would like to thank Cheri Dean, Anastasia Spanhake, Chelsea Carr and Deb Palmer, who took the time to read my drafts and offer their wonderful insights and suggestions.

I would also like to thank the people of Vanguard Press, an imprint of Pegasus Elliot Mackenzie, for guiding me through the publishing process and helping me to share my passion with others.

Chapter 1

Darcy placed her key into the lock, turned the knob, and pushed against the door. It didn't open. She groaned and pushed harder, but it still wouldn't budge. She leaned her shoulder into it and used her body weight. The door flew open and she caught herself just before falling onto the floor. *You've got to be kidding me,* Darcy thought as she looked around the dim cabin. It was evident that no one had been there in years. A thick layer of dust and cobwebs were proof of that. She slid off her immaculate white pea-coat and groaned when she spotted a long smudge of ground in dirt running down her sleeve as a result of her attempt to get into the little cabin. *Just great.*

When Darcy had received a call from her mother's lawyer telling her that the estate had been settled, she was relieved. She had always been incredibly close to her mom and the last few months had been hell. Taking her mother to chemo appointments and watching her grow weaker was excruciating and Darcy had felt so helpless. Since her mom's passing, each day had been filled with making decisions and each night filled with an emptiness that wouldn't go away.

She had been surprised to learn that her mother had owned a cabin in West Forks, Montana and more so to discover that now it was hers. Her mother had never mentioned the cabin and from what she could see she understood why. Darcy turned around and walked back out the door. The first order of business was to drive back into town and buy some cleaning supplies. There was no way she was going to put her belongings in a place that looked like that.

She climbed back into her Mustang convertible. The temperature had gotten much warmer in the past few hours, and now she could finally put the top down. She loved driving with the wind blowing through her hair and she didn't feel the least bit guilty for splurging money on her car. Once she'd become a successful blogger, this car had been her first indulgence.

Darcy pulled into the little town of West Forks and groaned. This town was a long way from the bustling city of Seattle where she called home. She parked in front of a general store and ignored the parking meter noting that her car was the only one on the deserted street. She doubted she'd be more than ten minutes in the quaint little store. She walked up the creaky wooden steps leading to Sally's general store. She pulled open the screen door and then pressed down on the metal latch of the handle to open the solid wooden door. *Where the hell am I?* she had asked herself on more than one occasion today.

The door creaked when she walked in and a little bell chimed letting the person working behind the counter know that she was there. An older woman looked up and smiled. Darcy forced a smile towards the woman and began walking down the aisles looking for cleaning supplies.

"May I help you?" the woman asked, looking in Darcy's direction.

Darcy scanned the room and asked, "Where do you keep the cleaning supplies?" The woman replied, "You're standing right in front of them." Darcy looked in front of her and didn't see anything but cooking supplies. She rolled her eyes and began walking again. The woman was obviously going to be no help at all.

The bell over the door chimed again and Darcy saw a tall, rugged, handsome man walk through the door. "Hi, Sally," the man said. "You're looking as pretty as ever."

Sally smiled at the man with her eyes twinkling. "Aw, Colin, you are a sweetheart. Your momma sure did raise you right."

Colin looked over and saw the curly dark-haired stranger looking flustered as she busied herself looking for something. He walked over to her. "You're not from around here, are you?"

Darcy looked up at him, annoyed. "What was your first clue?" She walked back up to the counter to ask Sally about the cleaning supplies again.

The man followed her. "Is that your blue 65 Mustang out front?" Darcy ignored the man and tried to focus on Sally. The man was unrelenting as he walked up to Darcy and held out his hand. "I'm Colin, and you are?"

Darcy looked up. "In a hurry and annoyed. Now if you'll excuse me, Sally was going to help me find what I need so I can be on my way."

Colin eyed her for a bit longer than Darcy felt was comfortable and then he said, "I put a dime in the meter for you. I'm sure it was an oversight since you are...how did you phrase it...In a hurry and annoyed?" He lifted his eyebrow. Darcy turned away and walked towards Sally.

Sally looked at Colin and rolled her eyes as she followed the irritated woman down the aisle. Darcy looked at Sally and gestured at the shelves, "I do not see any cleaning supplies. Do you happen to have some in the back?"

Sally stifled a laugh and said, "Ma'am, all you need is vinegar, baking soda, dish soap, and some water."

Darcy looked at her, baffled. "Please tell me you're kidding."

Sally shook her head. "No, I'm not. Do you know how many harmful chemicals are in the commercial stuff? No one around here buys that. It's easy to make. I can help you if you'd like."

Darcy looked at Sally like she was speaking in another language. She glanced around, exasperated, just as her phone rang. Darcy held up one finger to let Sally know she wasn't finished. "Hi, Emma honey. How's your first week at camp?" She listened to her daughter happily chatting away and then said, "I miss you too. I'll be looking for my first letter." She hung up her phone and then looked back at Sally as though they had never been interrupted. "Where is the nearest town that sells real cleaning supplies?"

Colin walked up and took off his cowboy hat. "That would be Springston, about twenty miles from here."

Darcy looked from one to the other. "You can't be serious."

Colin looked at her straight faced. "You don't seem the type that has a sense of humor. I'm not kidding."

Darcy rolled her eyes. "Mister—"

Colin interrupted. "The name's Colin, remember, I introduced myself to you."

Darcy blew out a breath. "Yes, you did. Colin, Sally, thank you for being so helpful. I will be on my way now. The name of the town is Springston, you said?"

Colin put his arm around Sally's shoulder and grinned. "Yes, it's that way," he said, pointing west.

Darcy nodded curtly and walked out the door.

Sally blew out her breath. "That's city folk for you."

Colin nodded and smiled. "Well, I'm sure she's just passing though and if not, she won't be here for long with an attitude like that."

Chapter 2

Darcy walked towards the cabin, her arms laden with bags of supplies and groceries. She balanced a bag on her hip as she slipped her key into the lock. She turned the knob and then pushed. She groaned when the door wouldn't budge. *Not again.* She stepped back, precariously balancing her bags, and then banged the door with her hip, forcing it to open. The door swung open and Darcy stepped inside and placed her bags on an old wooden table. The place didn't look any better the second time. *One thing at a time,* she reminded herself. She slipped off her jacket and groaned when she saw a much bigger dirt streak on her white coat to match her previous one.

Darcy pulled her unruly brown curls up into a ponytail and then rolled up her sleeves. She walked over to one of the bags and pulled out a spray bottle of cleaning solution. It felt like an accomplishment holding the bottle in her hand, given the experience she'd had at Sally's general store, and the nonsensical drive to another town just to get it. She pulled out a roll of paper towels, walked over to the kitchen counter and started to uncover the layers of dust and grime. As she was wiping down the counter, a dark figure passed by her window. She stopped cleaning and looked out. She didn't see anything. She walked out onto the porch and around the house, but still saw nothing. *It must be my imagination.* She walked back inside.

Darcy couldn't remember the last time she had scrubbed away at something. Her house cleaner, who came twice a week, took care of things like this. It wasn't that Darcy minded cleaning. It was more like Darcy didn't have time to clean since she started her own blog site and then started writing true crime thrillers in her spare time. Her blogging site had taken off and Darcy preferred to work or spend time with Emma than to spend her time cleaning.

A few hours later, Darcy stood back and admired her work. Everything in the kitchen sparkled and she marveled at the patterns in the woodwork of the solid oak cabinets and counter tops. She could tell that her grandfather had been a woodworker and had built this cabin and everything in it. She opened a bottle of water and took a sip. It tasted cool and refreshing amid all the dust and grime that wafted through the air. Her stomach growled, reminding her that she hadn't eaten dinner. Since the electricity wouldn't be turned on until tomorrow, her choice was the bag of potato chips she had picked up or venturing out to the local diner she had passed when she first drove into town. Neither one seemed particularly appetizing; she really missed elegant dishes made by real chefs.

She shifted her body and rolled her shoulders, trying to loosen the muscles that were starting to ache. She removed a dusty floral sheet that covered the couch and was surprised to see that it looked like new. She sank down on the couch and could feel her body relax. She closed her eyes and drifted off to sleep, until her stomach started growling again. She wiped her eyes and saw that the cabin was dark. She looked around and froze when she saw the shadow of a person standing in the corner watching her. She screamed and threw her book at the shadow. It didn't move.

"Who are you?" she shouted in a shaky voice. Still nothing. Her heart raced. She didn't want to die. She pleaded, "Take what you want. There's money in my purse, just take it and go. Please don't hurt me." She was crying now. The shadow remained in the corner unmoving. She slid her hand between the couch cushions hoping she would find something she could use to defend herself. Her heart sank when she felt nothing there. She was defenseless. She felt lightheaded and nausea began roiling through her body. Still the shadow didn't move. With a trembling hand she reached for her phone and turned on the light. If she was going to die, she would die fighting. She pointed the light toward the corner. There stood a mannequin with a knife stuck in its chest. She couldn't breathe and for a moment she thought she'd pass out. She took a deep breath, trying to calm her racing heart, now that she knew the shadow wasn't real.

When her body stopped shaking, she quickly walked over to the bag that held candles, lanterns and batteries. She put the batteries in the lantern and could finally see. She grabbed a kitchen knife from a drawer as she felt sweat roll down between her shoulder blades. She slowly and silently walked through the cabin looking for the intruder. When she was certain no one was hiding inside she walked outside.

"What do you want!" she screamed. There was no answer. Satisfied that no one was there, she entered the cabin and braced herself for the mannequin once again. It was gone.

She reached for her cell phone to dial 911 but remembered she didn't have any cell service or a landline. Plus, who would believe her? She didn't have any proof now that the mannequin had disappeared. It was probably just some local kids playing a prank on her because she wasn't from around here.

Darcy lit the candles to create more light in the room. The reflection of the flames danced off the newly polished counters. She didn't like people playing tricks on her and she'd be damned if they scared her off her own property. She glanced out the window one last time, double checked that all the windows and doors were locked, then carried her lantern back over to the couch. She kept the kitchen knife close by just in case and picked up the book lying on the floor. She lay on the couch and started reading. It was nearly dawn before she finally drifted off to sleep.

Chapter 3

Darcy pulled up in front of Frank's Diner and stepped out of her car. She walked through the door and every patron stopped eating and stared at her. Darcy ignored the stares and walked to a booth in the far corner. She was delighted to see there was an outlet along the wall. She plugged in her laptop and waited for it to boot up. She could see from the corner of her eye people looking her way and whispering.

A middle-aged waitress with a long blonde ponytail walked towards her with a menu.

"Can I get you some coffee?" she asked as she placed the menu down in front of Darcy.

Darcy smiled up at her and said, "I assume you don't serve lattes?"

The blonde waitress pasted on a smile and patiently said, "No, ma'am, we don't but we make a great cup of coffee."

Darcy tried to hide her disappointment. "Coffee would be fine. I'd also like an order of scrambled eggs with bacon and toast, please."

The waitress reached for her menu. "Okay, I'll put in your order." A few minutes later she returned holding a pot of fresh coffee and filled Darcy's cup.

"Excuse me," Darcy said, looking up, "do you have a Wi-Fi password so that I can connect to the internet?"

The waitress rolled her eyes and said, "We don't typically give it out."

Darcy took a deep breath and put on her best smile. "I know I'm being a bit of a pain but I'm in a tough spot here. You see, I do a daily blog and my readers are expecting something new from me." In a last-ditch effort she said, "I'm an excellent tipper."

A young teenage girl sitting at the next table looked over and asked, "What's your blog about?"

Darcy smiled in relief, someone who was in touch with the real world and knew what a blog was. "I review different products and give my opinion to my readers."

The mother of the teenage girl looked over and said, "People actually read those and follow your advice?"

Darcy put her napkin in her lap as her breakfast was served. "Well, everyone might not follow my advice, but many do." The waitress slipped her a piece of paper which held the Wi-Fi password and winked. "Thanks!" Darcy said with relief, as she started typing it into her computer.

The bell chimed over the door as a police officer entered the diner. He walked up to the counter and took a seat as the waitress poured him a cup of coffee. "Thank you, Miranda. I'll just have the special today."

Miranda filled out an order ticket and stuck it in the window then she busied herself with her other customers. The officer looked around and spotted Darcy, vigorously typing on her computer. He grabbed his cup of coffee and walked over to her.

"Good morning, Darcy," he said, smiling. Darcy was startled at hearing her name and looked up. It was Colin, dressed in uniform, and smiling smugly at her.

She glared at him. "How do you know my name?"

Colin sat down uninvited and said, "We met yesterday at the general store remember? I introduced myself."

"And I didn't," Darcy reminded him.

Colin sat back and pretended to be thinking. "As a matter of fact, you didn't introduce yourself. That may be the way folks act back in Seattle, but in West Forks when someone is trying to be friendly the sentiment is usually returned."

Darcy quickly shut her computer and grabbed her purse. "Are you stalking me?" she asked, loud enough for the other diners sitting around them to hear.

A man from two booths over said loudly, "Colin, leave the girl alone. She ain't hurtin nothin."

Colin looked at the diners and asked, "What? I'm just doing my job."

The man glared at Colin. "And what's that, terrorizing new visitors that have come to our great town?"

Darcy stood quietly while the two men exchanged words. The other diners were watching with interest. "I'm the sheriff," Colin replied, exasperated. "It's my duty to know everything that goes on in this town. I was just checking her out, is all, to make sure she didn't have any outstanding warrants."

The whole diner laughed.

"Look at her, Colin. Does she look like a menace to society? If she does then, boy, you need glasses," Miranda replied from behind the counter. The diner erupted again in a fit of laughter.

Colin knew it was no use. He pulled a few bills from his pocket and threw them on the counter. "Keep the change," he mumbled to Miranda and then he walked out the door.

Darcy slipped on her coat and pulled the strap of her computer case over her shoulder. She walked towards the man who had come to her rescue and stopped at his table. "Thank you for defending me."

The man looked up from his newspaper and smiled. "You're welcome, young lady. I hate to see an innocent person such as yourself being badgered by our local sheriff. He means well but sometimes he goes a bit overboard, if you know what I mean."

Darcy breathed out a sigh of relief and smiled. "Well, once again, thank you."

The old man gestured to the seat across from him. "I'd like it if you would have a cup of coffee with me. I get tired of seeing the same faces day in and day out."

Darcy really wanted to get away from these locals who probably thought Frank's Diner was a five-star restaurant, but she could hear her mother berating her rudeness and she didn't need any more enemies. "I'd love to," she smiled, and slid into the booth across from him. The old man held his hand out across the table and said, "The name's Jack."

Darcy reached for his hand and shook it. "I'm Darcy Blackwell. It's nice to meet you."

Jack studied Darcy and asked, "So, Darcy from Seattle, what brings you to West Forks?"

Darcy was hesitant to bring up the fact that she was staying in a cabin alone in the middle of the woods and was about to make up a story until she looked into Jack's eyes and knew she couldn't lie. "My grandparents, or I should probably say my grandparents' estate."

Jack narrowed his eyes and looked straight into Darcy's. "I don't recollect anyone passing away recently. Who were your grandparents?"

Darcy shifted uncomfortably and tried to change the subject. "Why don't you ask Colin? He seems to know a lot about me."

Jack laughed. "Honey, he just ran your plates. He takes his job as sheriff seriously, in fact too serious if you ask me. So back to the question, who were your grandparents?"

Darcy looked uncomfortable answering the question but knew Jack wasn't going to let up. She waved at the waitress for her check and then looked back at Jack. "I'm not really sure what their names were."

Jack looked unconvinced. "Let me get this straight. You don't know who your grandparents were, but you are here because of their estate?"

Darcy smiled as Miranda walked up with the check then looked back at Jack. "I know it sounds crazy, but I've never met them. My mother moved away before I was born."

Jack leaned back and studied Darcy. Miranda took Darcy's money and carried it to the cash register.

"Would your grandparents happen to own a cabin up on Nintauk Lake?"

Darcy looked surprised. "Yes, that would be the one."

Miranda arrived back at the table with Darcy's change.

"Well, I'll be," said Jack, leaning back in astonishment.

Miranda looked at both Darcy and Jack. "Is everything all right, Jack?"

Jack continued to look at Darcy. "Now I see the resemblance, you're Kimberly Wickett's daughter, aren't you?"

Darcy shifted uncomfortably in her seat, looking from Miranda to Jack.

"My mother's name was Kimberly Blackwell."

Now it was Miranda's turn. "Oh. My. Stars! I never knew Kim had a daughter."

"You knew my mother?" Darcy asked in astonishment.

"Knew her?" Miranda replied. "We were best friends." The bell chimed above the door and two more customers walked in. Miranda looked at Darcy and said, "Well, looks like I've gotta take care of old Henry and Muriel. Maybe we can catch up later?"

Darcy smiled, "I'd like that."

Miranda walked over as Henry pulled out Muriel's chair and helped her get seated. Miranda put her arm around Henry's shoulder and said, "Henry, you sure could teach my husband a thing or two about spoiling the love of your life."

Henry smiled and said, "Miranda, darlin, it's not spoiling, it's called love. Even after fifty years of marriage I'd still do anything for Muriel and that's no lie." He walked over and took a seat across from his wife and placed their order without even looking at the menu.

Darcy looked back at Jack and smiled. "Okay, Jack, now that we've figured out who I am, tell me something about you."

Jack looked surprised at her question and said, "Ain't much to tell. I'm just a grumpy old timer who's lived here most of my life."

Darcy said, "Why do I get the feeling there's more to you than what you're letting on?" She waited but she could tell Jack wasn't going to be more forthcoming. She looked down at her watch and knew she wanted to get back to the cabin. "Well, Jack, you don't seem grumpy to me. It was nice meeting you and thank you again for coming to my rescue. Hopefully, I can stay away from Colin, so this doesn't happen next time."

Jack laughed. "Let me give you some advice about Colin. He's a lot like his father. He's stubborn and pigheaded and once he gets an idea in his head he won't let go until he's satisfied. I have a feeling you'll be seeing him again."

Darcy groaned, collected her belongings, and walked towards the door. She climbed into her car and started it up. Every time the engine revved, her heart still fluttered. She slipped her sunglasses over her eyes and began the drive back toward the cabin. She hoped the electricity would be on by now and there were no more surprises. She turned left down the private road that led to the tiny log cabin and slowed down as she drove over the uneven ground. She looked at the tall ponderosa pine trees lining both sides of the gravel road. She felt so small and insignificant in comparison. She was surprised that her mother had never mentioned the cabin, even when she was in her last stages of cancer. Darcy couldn't have been more surprised when the lawyer informed her that she was now the owner.

She looked at the cabin now that it was lighter outside and saw that much of the outside repairs were only cosmetic; Nothing that re-staining and paint wouldn't fix and, of course the door, needed to be fixed. She pushed against the door as she unlocked it and was surprised that it opened the first time. She went inside and tried the light switch. The lights flickered at first and then stayed on. She went over and plugged in the stove and refrigerator, hoping they still worked after all this time. They were both out of date, but as long as they worked Darcy would be happy. She knew she should start cleaning out the rest of the cabin, but the sun was shining, and it was too nice to stay inside on a day like today. She switched out of her sneakers and put on her hiking boots. She rolled up the sleeves on her flannel shirt and tied her curls into a ponytail.

Darcy stepped out the back door onto an old rickety deck. The wood felt weak in places and she knew she would have to replace it sooner rather than later.

The grass in the yard was overgrown and looked more like a hay field than a yard. She could see the lake beyond the tall grasses. She gingerly walked across the deck and down the stairs. Once she was on safe ground, she started to hike through the grass and weeds towards the lake. It was more work than she had first anticipated. The overgrown brush was dense in places and pushing her way through it was more than she had bargained for. She also hadn't counted on the briars and thickets of blackberry bushes along the way.

She was rewarded as she finally stood at the edge of the lake. The reflection of the trees bouncing off the still water was breathtaking. Darcy wiped the sweat off her brow and looked up. The sun had risen higher. She took off her heavy boots and stuck her feet into the water. It was cool and felt refreshing. She eyed the wooden pier that was leading out farther into the water.

It didn't look very sturdy from where she stood. She rolled up her pant legs and waded out a little farther. The crystal-clear water was so tempting. She wished she could take a quick dip to cool off. She was surprised to discover that she was enjoying the seclusion. Normally, she loved the hectic life that came with living in a bustling city.

She knew that the lake was on the one hundred acres of property that she now owned which meant that there wouldn't be anyone around. She laughed at herself as she spontaneously slipped off her clothes and waded out farther into the water, she kept going until she had to swim to stay afloat. She loved the serenity and the freedom to just let go of all the stress and sadness from the last few months. She continued swimming, enjoying the feel of the water gliding over her body.

"Ahem! Darcy, is that you?" came a voice from the shore.

Darcy froze and prayed she was imagining this. She slowly turned around and saw Colin standing on the shore holding his hat in his hands. She cleared her throat and yelled across to him angrily, "Colin, why are you here?"

Colin tried to keep his eyes on Darcy's and not drift to her bare body just beneath the water. "I could ask you the same thing," Colin shouted to her.

"This really isn't any of your business," Darcy retorted.

Colin grinned. "I'm the sheriff, remember? Everything that goes on in this town is my business."

"This is beyond ridiculous," Darcy retorted. "Can you walk over by those trees and turn around so I can get out of the water and get dressed?"

Colin shook his head and smiled smugly "Now, how do I know you won't try to flee?"

Darcy was seeing red. "Fine, Sheriff, have it your way." Darcy started walking out of the water and Colin's throat went dry. He turned his back before he said or did something stupid. "What's the problem, Sheriff? I thought you were afraid I'd flee?"

Colin grimaced with his back still turned away from Darcy. "I may have exaggerated just a bit. Are you dressed yet?" There was no answer. Colin cleared his throat. "Darcy are you decent?" Still no answer. He turned around and saw that Darcy was stomping off back towards the cabin. "Wait up," he yelled. Darcy didn't turn around but kept walking. Colin caught up to her just as she was stomping up the steps of the porch to go inside. He shouted, "I wouldn't do that if I were you. You are trespassing on private property and I will charge you for trespassing and obstruction of justice."

Darcy shook her head, getting more aggravated by the minute and walked into the cabin. Colin followed her inside just as Darcy grabbed some papers and shoved them at his chest. He lifted an eyebrow, looking at her and then at the papers. It was the deed to the cabin along with a copy of the will. When Colin had finished reading, he handed them back to her.

"Why didn't you just tell me?" he asked.

Darcy glared at him. "Because it isn't any of your business." She crossed her arms in front of herself, trying not to shake in anger. "How did you know I was here anyway? You're stalking me, aren't you."

Colin laughed. "Sweetheart, you are quite full of yourself. I have better things to do with my time. I stopped here because I saw fresh tire tracks leading to the cabin and I knew this cabin had been deserted for years."

Darcy stepped closer to him and narrowed her eyes. "Well, it's not deserted any more, and you, sir, are trespassing on my property. I would like it if you would leave."

Colin shook his head in disbelief and looked amused. "Yes, ma'am," he said, putting on his hat. "You know, none of this would have happened if you would have just been up front when we met, instead of being so secretive."

Darcy balled her hands into tight fists, trying to keep from being arrested for assaulting a police officer. She stepped closer and poked Colin in the chest as she enunciated each word. "I. Am. None. Of. Your. Business."

Colin looked into her steely eyes and tipped his hat. "I'll be seeing you, Darcy." He sauntered out the door and into his car. He stuck his hand out in a wave as he drove away.

Chapter 4

Darcy turned on the lights, once again thankful for working electricity, and opened the refrigerator to grab a bottle of cold water. She looked around the cabin at all the cleaning she still had left to do, but surprisingly it had already begun to feel cozy. She was still amazed by all the intricate woodwork that was done by hand. Today, she decided, she would tackle the bedroom so that hopefully she would have a bed to sleep in tonight.

Darcy pulled all the linens from the bed and put them in the laundry basket. She also pulled off all the old, faded sheets that were covering the furniture. She looked in amazement at the hand-carved desk that her grandfather must have built for her grandmother. It was beautiful. Darcy carefully opened the top drawer and saw a stack of letters rubber banded together. She was surprised to see the first letter was addressed to her mother, with the red letters 'Return to Sender' stamped across the front. As she leafed through the letters, she was astonished to see that all the letters were addressed to her mother and all had been stamped in the same way.

Darcy slipped her finger under the flap of the envelope that laid on top and opened it. She carefully pulled out the yellowing paper and began to read.

Dear Kim,

I know you are angry with your father and me for refusing to give Tommy our blessing for your hand in marriage. I also know that you are stubborn just like us and will do things your own way. We love you, Kim, and we only want the best for you. Please come home.

Love,
Mom

The lights began to flicker and then they went out. Her mind raced when she thought of the events of last night. She listened intently but heard nothing. She let out a frustrated groan. Her imagination was getting the best of her. She walked into the kitchen, opened the cabinet drawer for a lighter and lit a candle. Then she grabbed the lantern, turned it on, and walked over to the fuse box. She clicked through each fuse, but nothing came back on. *This is ridiculous,* she thought. *I'm going to have to drive all the way back to that po'dunk town just to call the electric company.*

Darcy reached for her keys then thought of Colin. She groaned. She didn't want to face him, not again. She laid her keys back down on the counter and walked over to the window. She pulled back the drapes and light penetrated the darkness. She checked her watch; she still had a few hours before dusk. She walked back over to the desk and picked up the letter again. Darcy studied the date and saw that it was dated 1984. That would have made her mother seventeen at the time. She wondered why her mom would want to get married so young and why didn't her grandparents like Tommy? Darcy picked up the next letter and then the next one. Each letter left her with more questions than answers. The biggest question of all was: why did all these letters come back unopened?

She didn't have any answers but knew someone who might. Darcy changed into her favorite pair of jeans and a white tank top with a denim shirt over it. She hastily brushed through her curly hair and grabbed her keys. Before she left, she made sure that all the doors and windows were locked tight. She looked up at the bright sunny sky and smiled, feeling better than she did earlier. She took a deep breath of clean mountain air as she put down the white convertible top, secured it, then climbed inside and started the car. It didn't take long for her to pull up in front of Frank's Diner. She quickly looked around, praying that Colin wasn't lurking nearby ready to pounce. She smiled when she spotted Miranda standing behind the counter reading the newspaper in the empty diner.

Darcy smiled. "Hi Miranda."

Miranda looked up. "Oh hey, Darcy. You can sit wherever you'd like. Are you here to use the internet?"

Darcy laughed and shook her head. "Not today. I was hoping to use your phone. My electric went out."

Miranda pointed Darcy to the phone. Darcy placed her call and then walked towards the table she'd sat at the last time she was there. It was nestled in a corner and the privacy would be nice in case other customers came in. She sat down as Miranda walked over holding a fresh pot of coffee.

"Coffee?" she asked.

Darcy smiled. "I would love some. You read my mind. Umm, Miranda can I ask you something?"

"Sure."

Darcy wasn't sure where to begin. "This might take a while. Would it be possible for you to sit and talk?"

Miranda looked around at the empty diner and sighed. "I suppose I could squeeze you in."

Darcy laughed. "Thank you."

Miranda sat down across from Darcy and poured herself a cup of coffee. "What do you want to know?" she asked.

Darcy began, "I found a stack of letters in my grandmother's desk. They were all addressed to my mom and they were all returned unopened. In many of the letters my grandmother keeps talking about someone named Tommy. Do you know who he is?"

Miranda looked confused. "Sugar, that's your dad. You have his last name."

Darcy shook her head. "That's not right, my dad's name was Derek."

Miranda nodded her head, agreeing with Darcy. "Yes, his full name is Derek Thomas Blackwell, but

folks around here have always called him Tommy."
Darcy frowned. Miranda looked surprised. "How could
you not know this? Wasn't he around when you were
growing up?"

Darcy shook her head. "My mom said he was killed
in an accident."

Miranda reached over and grabbed Darcy's hand.
"Oh honey, I'm so sorry. I didn't know."

Darcy smiled sadly. "Thanks, Miranda."

Miranda took a sip of her coffee. "How's your
mama?"

Darcy's eyes started welling up. "She passed away
three months ago. She had cancer."

Now it was Miranda's turn to start crying. "Oh
sugar, I'm just asking all the wrong questions. I am so
sorry! Your mama and I were best friends. Oh, the
stories I could tell."

Darcy dried her eyes and smiled. "I'd love to hear
them sometime. My mom and I were always close."

Miranda smiled. "What would you like to know?"
Darcy leaned back in her chair. "Well, for starters, why
did my mom leave home at such a young age and never
contact her parents after she left?"

Miranda blew out a long breath. "How much time
do you have? This will be a long story."

Darcy looked serious and replied. "I've got all the
time in the world."

Miranda stood up, "Give me a minute, okay?" She
turned and walked into the kitchen and came back

carrying two pieces of lemon meringue pie. She put one down in front of Darcy. "This was your momma's favorite."

Miranda topped off their coffee and then started to talk. "Your mama and Tommy started dating in tenth grade. Tommy had just moved here, and your momma was head over heels for that boy the minute he stepped into our classroom." Miranda shook her head as she recalled the memory. "At lunch time Kim just walked right up and plopped down at the table across from him. They were inseparable after that. Your grandfather didn't like him much. Tommy had a mean streak and was always getting into fights. Your grandfather was sure he would end up in jail someday, but your momma was always defending him. Kim was always talking about getting out of this little hick town and marrying Tommy. One night Kim and your grandparents got into another argument about him. They had seen bruises on Kim's arm and figured Tommy was hitting her. She denied it and said Tommy had never touched her, but your grandparents didn't believe any of it. Your grandpa got in his truck to go after Tommy, but Kim stopped him by promising to never see Tommy again. A few nights later, Kim left a note saying she was leaving with Tommy and not to look for her. I wasn't surprised. Kim would have followed Tommy to the ends of the earth. Anyway, your grandparents were heartbroken, especially your grandma, and they called the police. Since your mom had left a note and everyone in town knew the feud going on between your grandparents and your mom, the police declared her a runaway and didn't look too hard for her after that."

"That is so sad," Darcy remarked. "How did my grandmother know where to send the letters?"

Miranda was quiet for a minute, looking perplexed, and replied, "I don't really know if she did. There were rumors that she had hired a private investigator to track her down, but I can't say for sure."

Darcy thought about this. It was as though they were talking about a stranger and not her mother. It was all so surreal. "Miranda, what can you tell me about my grandparents?"

Just then the bell over the door chimed and two customers walked in. "Sorry, Darcy, I've got to get back to work, but if you see Jack, ask him. He and your grandfather were best friends and served in Vietnam together."

"Thanks for all your help, Miranda. Oh, I have one last quick question. The date on the letter was 1984, which is the year I was born. Do you know if she was pregnant?"

Miranda smiled and waved at the customers as they seated themselves then she looked at Darcy. "If she was, she never told me, but I do know they were intimate, so I guess it was possible."

Miranda walked over to the couple and Darcy watched as she took their drink order. It was obvious that Miranda knew the couple. Darcy had never lived in a place long enough to know many people. She had lived in big cities all her life and moved every couple of years. She never understood why her mother didn't want to stay in one place. She had asked her mom about it once and her mother had laughed and twirled Darcy around in the yard and said, "Darcy, life is short and there's just too much to see. If we stayed in one place, you'd never see what was out there." Then they would both lay down in the lush green grass pointing out clouds that looked like animals. Darcy never doubted that her mother had loved adventure. When Darcy got older moving no longer felt like an adventure and she dreaded the day when her mother would announce that they would be moving, again.

In hindsight, Darcy really couldn't complain. The experience of moving frequently had allowed her to see much of the United States and she had friends from all over. Of course, all that ended when her mother was diagnosed with cancer two years ago. Now, Darcy called Seattle, Washington home and she was determined to stay there for her daughter's sake.

After her conversation with Miranda, Darcy thought about the date on the letter again and wondered once again, if her mom had run away because she was pregnant?

With no one to keep her company, Darcy pulled her computer out of her bag and logged onto the internet. She couldn't work from the cabin since she still didn't have any service, but she could work at the diner, thanks to Miranda. Miranda wandered back over to Darcy and topped off her coffee. "What are you working on?" she asked curiously.

Darcy looked up. "I'm working on my blog. I try to keep it updated every couple of days. Plus, I'm checking my email since I just picked up a freelance job creating advertisements online. I'm waiting to hear back from a client."

"Wow, you are one busy tech savvy lady," Miranda replied and nodded towards Frank. "Frank could use some advertising advice. Things have slowed down in the past few years."

Darcy smiled. "I'd be happy to help." She could see Miranda's wheels spinning.

"I'll let him know." She walked off and left Darcy to her work.

The bell jingled over the door as Jack walked in. He looked around and sat down in his usual booth. Darcy looked over at him and smiled. "Hi, Jack. It's good to see you again."

Jack looked at Darcy and laughed. "People say a lot of things about me but being happy to see me is usually not one of them."

Darcy giggled. "I don't believe that for a minute. Can I buy you a cup of coffee?"

The look of surprise on Jack's face was priceless. "Sure. Would you like to join me?"

Darcy closed her computer and slid it back in her bag. "I would love to," she said, grinning. She grabbed her coffee cup and carried it over to Jack's table, just as Miranda popped over with Jack's coffee.

He sat back in his booth and looked at Darcy. "So, are you getting settled in at the cabin?"

Darcy groaned. "That'll take a while. I don't think anyone has lived there for several years."

Jack shook his head. "Not since your grandfather passed."

Darcy studied Jack. "Did you know my grandfather very well?"

He laughed. "You could say that. We fought in the Vietnam War. We were in the same battalion. We always watched each other's backs. Your grandfather was one ornery stubborn old cuss, and I was always glad I was on his good side."

Miranda walked over to their table and placed two plates of hot apple pie topped with vanilla ice cream in front of each of them. They both looked up in surprise. Miranda smiled. "My treat," she said, then she sauntered off.

Darcy looked back at Jack as he cut into his pie. "I've never met my grandparents. My mother told me they were both killed in a car accident when she was a teenager. She said she married my dad shortly after." Jack was quiet as he sipped his coffee. Darcy noticed and said, "I know they didn't die in a car accident. I found a bunch of old letters that my grandmother wrote to my mom over the years and they all said return to sender."

Jack nodded, "Your grandparents were good people. Strong willed and hardworking, but like I said, your grandfather was a stubborn ole cuss and you didn't want to see the wrong side of him. Unfortunately for Tommy that was the only side he saw, especially when there were rumors that he had gotten your mother pregnant." He looked at Darcy and said, "I don't pay no mind to small town gossip. I've got better things to do with my time, but I will say that Tommy had a reputation and it wasn't good."

Darcy frowned. "So, I've been told." She looked at her watch and said, "I should probably go. The power went out in the cabin. I called the electric company and with any luck it'll be on by the time I get back."

Jack looked concerned. "Does that happen frequently?"

Darcy laughed. "I don't know, Jack, I haven't been here long. I'm still cleaning it out, remember?"

Jack smiled. "Your Grandpa Hank sure was proud of that cabin. He built it with his own two hands."

Darcy smiled. "I could tell. The woodwork is amazing." She picked up her bag and slung it over her shoulder. "See you around, Jack."

Darcy reached the door just as Colin walked in. He looked at her and tipped his hat. "Darcy." Darcy rolled her eyes, pushed past him and made a beeline for her car.

Chapter 5

Darcy had just taken a break when she heard a knock at the door. She jumped when the sound broke the silence. She certainly wasn't expecting anyone and was hesitant to open the door after her electricity had mysteriously gone out earlier, then the mannequin prank before that. She didn't know anyone except for Miranda and Jack, and she had nothing for protection. She quickly looked around and grabbed a pair of scissors, just in case. She opened the door to see a nice-looking man in his thirties smiling at her. She noticed that his blue eyes crinkled when he smiled and those dimples, oh my. "Hello, are you Darcy Blackwell?" he asked.

Darcy looked at him warily. "Yes... and you are?"

The stranger replied, "My name is Adam Dixon. I was wondering if you had a couple of minutes to talk. I'd like to make you an offer that I think you'd be very interested in."

Darcy tried to hide her annoyance. "Thanks, but no thanks. I'm not interested in buying anything." She started to shut the door.

Adam spoke louder before the door closed completely, "How does one-point-two million dollars sound?"

Darcy stopped and opened the door wider. "What did you say?"

Adam looked at her seriously and repeated, "I said, I am prepared to give you one-point-two million dollars."

Darcy knew this was a joke. How could it not be? She didn't have time for this. But, then again, she'd just inherited a cabin she didn't know about. Maybe this was another inheritance. She wasn't convinced but she decided to hear him out.

She remained in the doorway, unsure if she wanted to let him in. "How did you know my name and where I lived? I haven't been here for very long."

Adam laughed. It was a deep throaty laugh and as much as she hated to admit it, she liked it. "I'm sorry," he said. "I can understand your hesitancy. I found you through the rumor mill of small-town gossip. When someone new is in town they are practically a celebrity."

Darcy smiled and rolled her eyes. "Of course. I'm not used to small town living yet. What's this about an offer that I can't refuse?"

Adam lifted up his briefcase and said, "Would it be all right if I came in? I have some paperwork to show you."

Darcy hesitated for a brief second, but he seemed harmless enough. She shrugged. "Sure, come on in."

Adam looked around the tiny cabin. "This place is… uh…cozy."

Darcy laughed. "Is that a polite way of saying small?"

Adam laughed. "Okay, you caught me. It's nice but a little small for my taste. I prefer more space and living in civilization."

Darcy looked at him quizzically. "I thought you lived in West Forks?"

Adam shook his head. "No, I'm just here visiting. I'm actually from Billings."

Darcy looked surprised. "Oh, I had just assumed you lived here. What brings you to West Forks?"

Adam's blue eyes pierced Darcy's. "You did." He placed his briefcase on top of the table and took out some paperwork. "I work for a company called Weston Enterprises and they are prepared to make you a very rich woman."

Darcy held up her hands. "Wait a minute. Why don't you start back at the beginning? Why are you here exactly?"

Adam leaned back in his chair. "Weston Enterprises is prepared to offer you one-point-two million dollars for your property here in West Forks."

Darcy stared at him stunned. She burst out laughing. "Okay, who put you up to this? This has got to be a joke. Who are you really?"

Adam handed her the paperwork and looked at her seriously. "As I stated earlier my name is Adam Dixon and I am here on behalf of Weston Enterprises."

Darcy took the papers that Adam was holding in front of her and looked at him annoyed. "I don't know who you are or who put you up to this but the jokes up and I want you out of my house."

Adam remained seated and tried to keep his temper under control. This was the most infuriating woman he'd ever met. "If you please just hear me out, I'd be happy to explain."

Darcy hesitated and eyed him suspiciously. Adam continued. "Weston Enterprises is a highly successful development company. They specialize in locating properties in rural areas and developing them which, as a result, brings revitalization and jobs to the community. The papers that you are holding are a legitimate offer to purchase your property."

Darcy put down the paperwork and asked, "How did they come to know about my property?"

Adam clasped his hands together and replied, "Weston Enterprises believes this town could benefit from revitalization, but they need a large amount of acreage in order to make that happen. You own a large amount of land and it is located close enough to town to make it convenient, yet far enough from town to give visitors a feeling of seclusion. This transaction would not only make you a rich woman, but it would also be a tremendous boost to the local economy of this town. Trust me, this would be a great opportunity for you and for them."

Darcy sighed. Her intuition was telling her not to take the deal. On the other hand, she thought of Miranda confiding in Darcy that Frank could use some help with advertising to bring in more customers. From what Darcy had noticed, business had been slow at the diner. She stood up. "Adam, you don't know anything about me so don't presume that you know what is best for me, but I will look over the offer and get back to you. Now, if there's nothing else, I'm quite busy and my time is valuable."

Adam looked startled and stood up, clicking his briefcase closed. He tried to muster a smile. "Great, read over the offer and think about it. My card is clipped to the top of the paperwork. As I said, this is the opportunity of a lifetime and—"

"Adam..." Darcy warned as she walked him to the door.

Adam coughed. "Right, don't presume. I'm sure...I mean I hope to hear from you soon."

Darcy felt the irritation begin to build back up inside her and she tried to control her voice. "I said I will look it over and I will. Adam, there's one more thing you should know about presumptions."

Adam groaned inwardly but pasted on a smile. "What is that?"

"Don't presume I'm stupid. This would be a great opportunity for Weston Enterprises. I'm merely a pawn that needs to be moved." Before he could respond she shut the door and locked it. Darcy didn't know why she was so irritated, the man was just doing his job, but she couldn't shake the feeling that something wasn't right. She placed the stack of papers on the old wooden mahogany desk that she had rescued from a thick layer of dust. She continued cleaning, thinking about what Adam had said. Oh, the things she could do with that kind of money, after all she wasn't planning on actually living here. Their home was in Seattle and if she did decide to keep the cabin it would be more of a getaway for when she needed a break. But for one-point-two million dollars, she could buy a house with an actual yard instead of the small apartment they were living in. Her daughter could finally have that dog she'd always asked for as long as Darcy could remember. The thought of Colin popped in her head. She smiled, she'd never have to see him again and that was a huge incentive to sell. She thought of the town, or what these people called a town. They could go on with their own little lives and she could go back to living in anonymity rather than everyone knowing her business. Why would anyone tell a total stranger where she lived? That thought alone would be a good reason to sell and move out of here.

She moved to the bedroom and started uncovering the dresser and piling up the linens to take to the laundromat. She opened one of the dresser drawers and found a manila folder lying at the bottom under a pile of socks. Darcy carefully opened it and pulled out a pile of emails from a private investigator.

Darcy sat on the bed and began to read through them. Miranda had mentioned that maybe her grandmother had hired a private investigator to keep tabs on Darcy's mother. Darcy was surprised to see not only clips of her mother's life but also a timeline of her own life in writing and in pictures. There was everything, from the time and place of her birth, to pictures of her growing up, as well as pictures of her parents. Darcy had never seen pictures of her father. Her mom said there had been a fire before she was born, and everything had been destroyed.

Darcy studied her dad, trying to discern what qualities she had inherited from him. She supposed her eyes and chin looked a little like his. She wondered what he had been like and for the first time in many years she felt the void where her father should be. Her mother had never remarried. She always said Darcy was all she needed.

She leafed through more emails and then picked up a newspaper clipping. The heading said, 'Domestic Violence Victim Fights Back' and there was a picture of two police cars with their lights on sitting in front of a tiny white house with black shutters. Darcy read the article in disbelief. Apparently, there had been a domestic abuse call from a neighbor and the cops were in transit to the house when Darcy's mother shot her father in the knee. The ambulance arrived and had taken them both to the hospital while the little girl stayed with neighbors. Darcy sat in shock. This was something she'd see on reality television, not something that happened in her life. She closed the folder. This was more than she could handle.

She put the papers back in the folder and closed the drawer. She walked out into the kitchen and opened a bottle of wine. She filled a glass and then walked out onto the front porch. She took a seat in her grandmother's rocking chair. The sun was shining, and the temperature had gotten a little warmer than this morning. It had been such an odd day. First Adam stopping by and now she had just found out things about her own family that she had never known. She took a sip and let her head tilt back, allowing the sun to shine on her face. She felt herself relax until she heard a car coming down the private gravel road.

She opened her eyes and groaned when she saw the black and white police car kicking up dust in its wake. It slowed to a stop in front of the house and Colin got out and slowly ambled up to her. *Great, just what I need.* "To what do I owe the pleasure, Sheriff?" Darcy asked sarcastically.

Colin pulled his hat down further to shade his eyes. "I was just checking on our newest resident. I don't like the fact that you don't have a phone or any way to contact someone if something were to happen."

Darcy let out a laugh and said, "You don't have to worry about me. I'm a big girl. I can take care of myself."

Colin walked up on to the porch and motioned towards the rocking chair. "Do you mind if I sit?"

She eyed him guardedly but said, "No I suppose not. Have a seat, Sheriff."

He sat down on the rocker and said, "Please, call me Colin."

"Would you like a glass of wine or a beer, Colin?"

He shook his head. "No, I'm still on duty. Thanks though." They were both quiet for a few minutes until Colin spoke again. "So, are you getting settled in?"

Darcy laughed. "Not hardly, I'm still digging out from under the dust. I really don't mind though. It's like I'm unwrapping a gift. Once the dust is gone, the woodwork is spectacular. Did you know that my grandfather built this cabin by hand? Jack was telling me that this morning."

Colin was silent for a moment and then spoke. "Darcy, don't get too close to Jack. He's untrustworthy and will only disappoint you. He's not the person you think he is."

Darcy studied him. "Why are you telling me this?"

He shrugged. "I just see you talking to him a lot and thought you should know."

Darcy looked at him skeptically. Colin felt his throat go dry. Darcy may be stubborn and aggravating, but damn, was she beautiful. Colin's thoughts went back to when he saw her at the lake, and he could feel his heart skip a beat. This was a path he couldn't go down, so he quickly changed the subject to something safer. "Are you staying here for good or just visiting?"

Darcy took a sip of her wine and let out a sigh. "I'm just visiting. I had no idea I even had family here or that they owned a cabin. Right now, I'm just trying to sort through it all. Something interesting happened today, though."

Colin looked at her in surprise. "What was that?"

Darcy looked at him and replied, "I had an unexpected visitor. Maybe you know him? His name is Adam Dixon? He said he works for Weston Enterprises."

Colin thought for a minute and said, "I don't recall anyone named Adam Dixon, but I have heard of Weston Enterprises. They're a development corporation, aren't they?"

Darcy nodded and said, "They want to buy this place and the land that goes with it."

He looked surprised. "Are you planning on selling it?"

Darcy sighed. "I don't know. It's like I just found a part of my heritage, but on the other hand they made quite a hefty offer."

Colin was quiet for a moment and then said, "Why don't I look into it and see what I can find out. I'll also check into Adam Dixon and see what turns up."

Darcy laughed. "Now you're back to jumping to conclusions, Sheriff. Adam seems legit, but I wouldn't mind knowing more about Weston Enterprises. If I do sell, I want to make sure it's in the best interest of this town."

Colin stood to leave. "I'm sure the town would appreciate that. I'll let you know what I find out. Until then, maybe you should think about running a phone line out here. You know, in case you need help or something."

Darcy smiled and thought about Adam just showing up randomly. "I'll put it on my 'to do' list."

Colin tipped his hat and returned to his car.

***

The next morning Darcy was sitting at her usual table in Frank's Diner with a steaming cup of coffee in front of her. She was working on her blog and was startled when she heard her name. Looking up, she saw Adam standing in front of her, smiling. She felt the hair on the back of her neck prickle and forced a smile back. "Hi, Adam, I'm surprised to see you so soon."

Adam motioned towards the empty bench across from her and she nodded so he sat down. "You looked so engrossed I didn't want to disturb you, but I wanted to apologize for the other day. I know I might have sounded a little arrogant and pushy, but I want you to know that I was just doing my job. I'm really a pretty nice guy once you get to know me."

Darcy saved her work and closed her laptop. "If there's anything we can agree on it's doing our jobs. In fact, I was just getting caught up on my emails and trying to get some work finished myself. As you may have guessed, there aren't many places that get service around here."

Adam held up his cell phone. "Oh, believe me, I've noticed." They both laughed. "So, I've got to ask, what on earth possessed you to live here?"

Darcy began to relax and shook her head. "I don't live here. I'm just tending to my grandparent's estate. I live in Seattle, Washington."

Adam nodded. "That makes more sense."

Darcy looked at him quizzically. "What do you mean?"

Adam grinned. "Just that a beautiful lady such as yourself deserves more than being stuck in a little hick town. There's nothing here. In the city you have so much more to do and see."

Darcy laughed. "When I first arrived, I thought the same thing, but now that I've met some very nice people and I've learned to slow down, it's really not that bad."

He didn't look convinced. "Aren't you scared staying up there all alone?" he asked. "Do you have a phone or anything?"

Darcy looked startled. "You're the second person to bring that up. Yes, I plan on having a phone installed out there."

The bell jingled over the door and Colin walked in. He smiled at Darcy, but his smile didn't last long when he saw a man sitting with her. He walked over to Darcy's table. "Hi, Darcy, who's your friend?"

Darcy looked up at Colin and rolled her eyes when she saw testosterone daggers shooting between the men. She cleared her throat. "This is Adam Dixon. I believe I mentioned him to you the other day and Adam, this is our local sheriff, Colin."

The two men sized each other up before Colin asked, "Where are you from, Adam?"

Adam took another sip of coffee. "Billings."

Colin nodded and studied Adam. "Are you here for business or pleasure?"

Adam looked over to Darcy and said, "A little of both I suppose."

Darcy smiled and said, "Sheriff, are you finished interrogating my friend?"

Colin's gaze moved from Adam and looked over at Darcy. *Since when had they become friends? She just met him the other day. He couldn't figure her out.* He looked back at Adam and tipped his hat. "I'll be seeing you around."

Adam looked back at Darcy. "He doesn't seem the friendly type."

Darcy laughed. "He just likes to know what's going on in this town. It's his job."

Adam let out a breath. "If you say so. Have you had a chance to look over the paperwork for the property? Are you getting any closer to a decision?" Darcy was about to go off on him again. He could see it in her face.

He put up his hands in surrender. "I'm asking off the record, as a friend, not as a representative of Weston Enterprises. I swear."

Darcy studied him a while and could tell he was being sincere. Darcy shook her head. "No, it's a big decision."

Adam laughed. "How can it be a big decision when you just inherited it and live in Seattle? Just think of all the things you could do for your daughter with that money."

Darcy looked at him in surprise. "I don't recall telling you that I had a daughter."

Adam looked chagrined. "Sorry, that's what I was told when the company sent me out here."

Darcy began to feel the hairs on the back of her neck prickling again. "Weston Enterprises probing into my personal life is not going to get them what they want. It'll get them the opposite. You leave my daughter out of this."

"It's not me, Darcy. It's the company that I work for. I will tell them, and I promise you that your daughter has nothing to do with this. Honestly, they just wanted to know who they were dealing with. They are just a company that wants to do a good thing for this town, although if you ask me, I have no clue what they see in this town."

Darcy calmed down. "What would happen if I agreed to the sale? What does Weston Enterprises plan to do with my property?"

Adam could feel himself relaxing again. "They plan on creating lodges around the lake. It would be a getaway resort for vacationers.

"Sounds impressive," Darcy replied. "I can see the kids swimming in the lake or playing in the snow."

Adam laughed. "Try picturing an adults' only resort with cross-country skiing and private hot tubs. Plus, let's not forget all the luxurious amenities that go along with an adults' only resort." Darcy listened but she didn't like what she was hearing. Adam continued. "Just think what you'd be doing for this town."

"What do you mean?" Darcy asked.

"What I mean," said Adam, taking a sip of coffee, "is look around you, Darcy. This diner is nearly empty, but with high end lodges drawing people here it would be full. Of course, there would be a change in menu and a Michelin star chef in the kitchen not to mention a major upgrade to the interior and exterior of the building. Imagine, pricey gift shops lining each side of the road, restaurants, probably a nightclub and other entertainment businesses. The amount of revenue that would come into this town would boost their economy drastically."

Darcy took a sip of coffee. "Huh, I hadn't thought of it that way." Although she didn't like the idea of an 'adult resort' she did like the possibility of helping the economy.

Chapter 6

Darcy parked in front of her house and groaned when she noticed that her garbage was strewn throughout the yard. *Great, I guess I need to get something more durable than a metal garbage can.* Darcy cleaned up the mess and then looked around for the can. She looked everywhere but it was nowhere in sight. *That's strange,* she thought. She walked around to the back of the cabin and along the edge of the woods. It was nowhere to be found. *It must be here somewhere.* Her search proved futile. "I really am beginning to hate rural living," she mumbled as she climbed back into her car and drove to the general store.

She walked in and spied Jack talking to Sally, who was standing behind the counter. They both gave a small wave to Darcy. She smiled and waved back and then walked to the back to find a heavier garbage can. She carried it to the counter and Sally began to ring it up. Jack eyed the can.

"Everything all right Darcy?"

Darcy blew out her breath. "Yes, everything is fine. Something got into the garbage and I can't seem to find my garbage can. So, I came to pick up another one and this time I'm making sure it's heavier than my last one."

Jack looked at the can and then back at her. "Wild animals are common around here. They usually tend to leave people alone, but you do have protection in case you need it right?"

Darcy laughed. "Yes, Jack, I have pots and pans to scare it away."

Jack wasn't laughing. "Do you own any type of firearm or know how to use one?"

"Jack, you're overreacting. I'm fine. It was probably just a raccoon or something."

Jack looked serious. "Don't underestimate the wild, Darcy. That's how people get hurt. You need a gun to protect yourself. If an animal is hurt or sick it will attack, and pots or pans will not help you much."

Colin had walked in at the tail end of their conversation. "Now don't go scaring the lady, Jack. That's a well-built cabin and all she has to do is go inside and give me a call. I'll be right there." Colin looked at Darcy. "You did call about having a phone installed, right?"

Darcy replied, "I'm calling first thing Monday morning." She looked at the scowls between the two men and then looked at Sally. "Well, thank you for all the advice but it's getting late and I should be heading home."

Colin looked at Jack and said, "You can't be going around encouraging people to go out and buy a gun when they know nothing about firearms. That's irresponsible and someone's going to get hurt."

Jack squared his shoulders, "Now, Sheriff, that girl is the granddaughter of a military brother. I have a responsibility to help her stay safe."

Colin glared at him. "Maybe if you paid as much attention to your own family, you would still have one." He turned around, threw open the door and left.

Darcy stopped the car in front of the cabin and looked in disbelief as the metal garbage can sat where it always did. *I'm going to catch these pranksters and when I do, they won't be laughing.* She angrily threw the trash that she had collected earlier into the can and made sure the lid was locked down. She walked into the house and felt a chill. She turned to the left and noticed that the living room window was wide open, and the drapes were blowing in the breeze. She felt uneasy. She knew she hadn't left any windows open because she had been extra vigilant to keep away intruders. She looked around the little cabin, hoping she wouldn't find anything. She hated the constant feeling of being in danger. When she was sure that nothing was lurking nearby, she closed the window and locked it. She thought about what Jack had said and decided he was right. First thing in the morning she would go find him at the diner.

She didn't sleep well that night as she kept imagining the worst. She finally gave up and climbed out of bed. She walked over to the dresser and pulled out the file again. She separated what she had already read and continued from there. She came across another newspaper clipping about her father and his face was front and center, looking back at her from his mug shot. She studied it for the first time and noticed that she had also gotten her dark hair and slim build from him. She went on to read that he was sentenced to nine years in prison. She wondered why her mother had never told her this. She could understand why her mom wanted to hide the fact that her father was abusive and was in prison, but that didn't excuse her mom from telling her that her father was dead. She had always wondered about her father, and to know that he'd been alive all these years dumbfounded her. She also resented the fact that father never sought her out.

She put the article back, wondering if getting a firearm was a good idea. Apparently, her mother knew how to use one, but she couldn't imagine ever shooting anyone or anything. Maybe she could buy one and not purchase any ammunition. She could just use it as a scare tactic. She'd talk to Jack in the morning and see what he thought.

***

She stepped into the diner and waved cheerfully at Miranda, who was standing at the counter talking to Colin. She looked around and spotted Jack sitting in a booth reading the paper. She walked over to him and asked, "May I join you?"

Jack smiled. "Of course, Darcy. How are you? Any more wild critters bothering you?"

Darcy sighed in relief. "Not that I know of." She decided not to bring up the open window or the fact that her garbage can had returned. *Maybe I'm being paranoid.* She looked at Jack. "I was thinking about what you said, about buying a firearm for protection." Jack nodded, listening intently as Darcy continued. "I'm not keen on the idea but I agree that I probably should have something to protect myself with all the wild animals running around."

Colin stood up from where he was sitting at the counter and walked over to where Darcy and Jack were talking. He interrupted their conversation. "I'm glad you're apprehensive, Darcy. You should be, but in all reality, the animals will leave you alone if you leave them alone. Unless they're feeling threatened, they won't bother you. I've lived here all my life and I can't recall a time when anyone was attacked by a wild animal."

Jack huffed and looked up at Colin. "Excuse me, Sheriff, but I believe the lady and I were having a private conversation. I don't appreciate you eavesdropping."

Colin glared at Jack then turned to walk back to his seat at the counter. Darcy watched Colin walk away, admiring his backside, and then blushed when she saw Jack watching her with amused interest. She coughed and then said, "Maybe Colin's right. It's not like I'm going to live here. I'm just here for a short while and I'm sure I'm just overreacting."

Jack shrugged. "I wouldn't recommend a firearm unless you're sure, Darcy. It can be dangerous if you don't know what you're doing. Just be aware of your surroundings, but I've gotta confess a pretty woman such as yourself staying up in that cabin all by yourself makes me uneasy."

Darcy smiled. "I'll have phone service on Wednesday. I'm sure I'll feel much better once I have a way to communicate with the outside world."

Jack laughed.

They continued talking as Colin stood up and left. He didn't look very happy. Darcy looked at Jack. "I get the feeling that you and Colin don't get along. Why?"

Jack shrugged and replied, "It's a long story and one which you really don't want to hear, trust me. Let's just say Colin and I don't quite see eye to eye and we are both stubborn."

Darcy looked at her watch and replied, "Really? I haven't noticed." They both laughed. "I really should get going. Thanks, Jack, for the advice and the company. I really appreciate it."

Jack took another sip of his coffee and picked his newspaper back up. "Any time."

Darcy parked her car in front of the cabin and warily looked around. Her garbage was in the can. She walked up to the front door and opened it. She peered inside and didn't see anything out of place. She walked inside and breathed a sigh of relief. The feeling was short lived when she noticed that the paperwork for the sale of the cabin had been moved from the desk to the center of her bed. She knew she hadn't moved it. She grabbed a knife out of the drawer and quietly walked towards the bedroom. Her heart was frantically beating, and she was shaking. She prayed that whoever had been there was long gone. She stood in the doorway with the knife held above her head ready to strike then she peered inside.

The stacks of papers were on the bed with the word signature highlighted. She turned her head, looking around, and her heart stopped when she looked at the mirror on her dresser. Written in bright red lipstick were the words: 'Sell Now While You Still Can!!!'

So, she hadn't been imagining things. She dropped the knife and shakily grabbed her keys, running to her car as if her life depended on it and peeled away. It was times like these when she wished she had a working phone.

Her tires squealed as she pulled up in front of the police station and walked inside. Colin looked up in surprise and stood up. "What's wrong Darcy?"

She could feel tears trailing down her cheeks and quickly wiped them away. Her teeth chattered as she tried to speak, and Colin knew that something was very wrong. She started shaking again as he led her to a chair and asked his deputy to get her a glass of water. She gladly accepted the water and took a sip.

Once she had calmed down, she said, "Someone was in the cabin."

Colin's eyes grew wide, but his voice remained calm. "How do you know this?"

Darcy's hands started to shake as she explained. "Well, my first clue were the papers I'm supposed to sign sitting on my bed instead of the table, but the next clue confirmed it. It was a message written on my mirror with lipstick that said, 'Sell Now While You Still Can!'"

Colin quickly took down her statement and could feel his blood begin to boil. He was ready to fly out of there and throttle the son of a bitch who was terrorizing her. No one did this and got away with it. He tried to keep his voice neutral and not give way to his anger. The last thing he needed to do was race out of here half-cocked without knowing all the details. That's how cops got killed.

"What do you think the message was referring to?" Colin asked, even though he had his suspicions.

Darcy looked at him and said, "I'm pretty sure it was a threat and Weston Enterprises wants me to sell. It's pretty apparent, don't you think?"

Colin nodded and then said, "Do you think Adam could have done this?"

Darcy shrugged. "I honestly don't know. I would have said absolutely not if it was yesterday, but now I'm not so sure. No one else knows besides you and Adam that I have an offer to sell the cabin."

Colin looked at her and said, "I'm going to check into Adam's whereabouts yesterday and I'll let you know if anything turns up. Is there anything else that has been going on that seems strange to you? Think, Darcy."

Darcy nodded. "Yesterday there was a window open and I know I didn't open it. I thought I was just being paranoid. There was also that first night when I arrived, and a mannequin appeared in my corner with a knife stuck in its chest."

Colin ran a hand through his hair and yelled at her in a fit of anger. "What? How could you not report this? What were you thinking, Darcy?"

Darcy shouted back, "I was thinking that I had no proof. The mannequin disappeared before I could take a picture of it. I wasn't positive about the window. I didn't think you'd believe me. I'm not stupid, Colin. I thought I could take care of it."

Colin took a deep breath and blew it out. "I'm sorry I yelled. I shouldn't have done that. I can see you're upset and…" He looked at Darcy. "I'm sorry that you thought you couldn't come to me for help. Can we call a truce? I'd like to help you."

Darcy hastily wiped a tear away that had slipped down her face. "I'd like that."

He cleared his throat and said, "Let's get a statement from you and then if you don't mind, I'd like to take a ride out there to look around and take some pictures."

Darcy grabbed her purse. "You can ride with me if you'd like."

Colin shook his head. "I'll take my car in case I get called out."

They both walked out of the police station and drove out to the cabin. Darcy got out of the car and still holding her keys she went to unlock the door. The door handle turned easily. She frowned. "That's strange, I know I locked the door behind me. Even though I was scared, I remember turning the lock."

Colin stepped next to her. "Stand back and let me go in first."

Darcy stood to the side as Colin took out his gun. He pushed the door open and yelled, "Police!" There was no sound and Colin slowly entered the cabin. He kept his gun cocked as he looked throughout the small cabin and then shouted, "Come on in, Darcy. It's all clear." He slid his revolver back into his holster as Darcy nervously walked in and looked around.

She felt terrified and stammered in a shaky voice, "I'm telling you Colin I locked that door."

Colin made a note in his notebook and said, "I believe you. Let's get a look at that mirror." Darcy led him into the bedroom and froze. The mirror was spotless as though it had never been written on. Darcy looked at Colin. "I'm not making this up, Colin, I know what I saw."

Colin could see she was physically shaken. "I could dust the place for prints but honestly I doubt I'm going to find any," he replied.

Darcy's eyes filled with tears, not so much from helplessness as from anger. "How dare someone come into my home and play a prank on me?"

Colin continued. "I have a feeling that this isn't a prank, Darcy. I'm going to have my deputy make frequent patrols of this area to scare off whoever this is." Colin noted the stack of papers sitting on the table. "What exactly did the message say again?"

Darcy took in a deep breath. "It said, 'Sell Now While You Still Can!' You do believe me, don't you?"

Colin kept walking around searching for any evidence. "Oh, I believe you, all right and from glancing at that stack of papers from Weston Enterprises, I'd say there's probably a connection." Darcy picked up the pile and handed them to Colin. "About seven years back or so this same company had tried to acquire several properties around here and weren't successful. By looking at this offer they're making you, I'd say they want this property pretty badly. Are you sure no one else knows about this besides us and Adam?"

Darcy replied, "No one. Adam was the one who came out to the cabin to make the deal. Do you really think it could be him?"

"I wouldn't jump to conclusions just yet, but he is someone I'm going to check out, along with Weston Enterprises."

They both turned when they heard a truck driving towards the house. It was the phone company. Colin breathed a sigh of relief and said, "Well at least you'll be able to call if anything else seems out of sorts." He eyed her apprehensively knowing that what he was about to say wasn't going to be received well. "Maybe you should stay in town for a few days until I can clear all of this up."

Darcy's eyes hardened. "I will not be bullied off of my own land and as far as Weston Enterprises is concerned, I've made up my mind, no deal."

Colin could feel his frustration build. "Darcy, I admire your bravery to want to stay here but until I clear this up, I don't think it's a good idea."

Darcy tried to still the nervousness in the pit of her stomach and appear confident as she said, "Thanks for the advice, Colin, and if anything else happens I'll give you a call."

Colin shook his head. "Okay, and like I said earlier, I'll have my deputy patrol out here to keep an eye on things."

Darcy ran a nervous hand through her hair, "Thanks. I'd appreciate that."

She walked back inside the house and locked the door. She walked through every room and made sure every window was locked too. She wasn't taking any chances. She checked her phone and found a dial tone. She finally felt her muscles start to relax as she made herself a hot cup of tea and grabbed a couple of cookies out of the cabinet. She still didn't have internet access, but she did have a good book, which she picked up and brought over with her to the couch. She threw a blanket over her lap and began to read until she fell asleep.

Chapter 7

The next morning Darcy woke to banging on her door. She tried to orient herself while simultaneously taming her erratic heartbeat. She hated living in fear like this. She stood up shakily and threw on the clothes lying on the floor that she had worn the day before. As she got dressed her fear turned to anger. She wasn't going to let anyone scare her off her own property. She refused to live in fear any longer. She walked into the kitchen and grabbed the largest knife she could find and then opened the door holding the knife in front of her ready to use it.

Colin was standing in her doorway and took a step back shocked when he saw the knife. He automatically put his hand on his gun without even thinking. Darcy dropped her hand and sighed with relief. "You scared the hell out of me!" she exclaimed. "Do you always pound on someone's door instead of just knocking?"

Colin relaxed and dropped his hand. "I tried knocking but there was no answer and I saw your car out front, so I knew you had to be here. Sorry if I scared you, but I just wanted to make sure you were okay. Did something else happen? Why are you holding a knife?"

Darcy grimaced, "Sorry, I wasn't expecting anyone, and I wanted to make an impression on whoever is terrorizing me. Come on in, I'll make you a cup of coffee."

Colin smiled. "That's kind of you, Darcy, but I'm just making my rounds. I've been thinking about you staying here alone and I'll be honest, I don't like it. I was wondering if you'd consider a compromise?"

Darcy looked at him suspiciously. "What kind of compromise?"

Colin grinned. "Stay right here, I'll be right back."

Darcy watched him walk back to his car and couldn't help but admire the muscular frame that was hidden under his well fitted uniform. He opened the door and held onto a leash. A German Shepherd hopped out of the back seat and walked obediently next to Colin. "Darcy, I'd like you to meet Rebel. He's about nine months old and he was training with our K-9 unit, but unfortunately, he's not meeting the qualifications and will no longer be able to continue training. He's very protective and once you get to know him, he's quite lovable. I was hoping if you'd consider giving him a home?"

Darcy was already in love; she knelt to pet the magnificent animal. Rebel wagged his tail. Colin held a ball for her to throw. Rebel darted after the ball and brought it right back to Darcy.

Colin cleared his throat. "Rebel will also help keep away wild animals and he's trained to stay beside you when you're outside so don't worry about him running off. Believe me, if anyone comes around, you'll know it." Darcy didn't like the idea of Colin thinking she couldn't take care of herself, but she admitted that it would be nice to have a dog around. She had always loved dogs and this one had already stolen her heart."

As she petted Rebel she tried to appear nonchalant. Her straight face hid her excitement. "Well, I'd hate to see him have to go to a pound since he didn't make the cut. I suppose I could keep him."

Colin grinned. "I was hoping you would. Thanks, Darcy. When they told me his name, I knew he was the one for you." Darcy rolled her eyes. Colin ignored her and said, "Well, I've got to get back to making the rounds. I'll be seeing you."

Darcy threw the ball for Rebel a few more times and then opened her door. Rebel walked inside and stayed right next to her. She walked over to the cabinet and took down a bowl and filled it with cold water. "Here you go, Rebel. You must be thirsty after all of that running." The dog lapped up the water eagerly and then walked over towards the couch where Darcy was sitting. He walked up to Darcy and put his head on her lap. She smiled. "Okay, Rebel, let's set some ground rules. You are a big dog, and this is a small couch. What if you lay on the floor next to the couch?" At the word "lay" Rebel automatically laid down. Darcy was impressed and she knew she loved him already.

"Well, I guess we're going to need some supplies, aren't we? You're a pretty big dog so I'm sure you have a hearty appetite. Plus, we'll need bigger bowls and toys. Feel like going for a ride?" At the word "ride" Rebel was up, wagging his tail, and walking quickly towards the door. "I guess I have room for you in the car. I'm guessing you'll want to ride shotgun, huh?"

Surprisingly, Rebel stopped by the back door of the car and waited patiently for Darcy to open it. She opened the door and the dog jumped in and sat down. Darcy started up the car and started driving towards town.

She pulled up in front of the general store and parked. Jack was walking lazily down the sidewalk. "What do you have in your car?" Jack asked, walking towards Darcy.

Darcy smiled. "Rebel," she said proudly. "Colin brought him by today and thought that maybe I'd like him to help keep the wild animals away plus keep me company at the cabin." Jack opened the door to pet him. At first Rebel growled. Darcy commanded, "Rebel, *no!*" He stopped growling and sniffed at Jack's hand.

"He seems more like a guard dog than a pet. Where did you get him?"

"Colin brought him to me. He said that Rebel wasn't meeting the qualifications for a K-9 dog and he needed a home."

Jack eyed Darcy. "He did, huh? That was nice of him."

Darcy knew the two men didn't get along so she tried to change the subject. "Jack, I've been thinking about what you said about learning how to shoot. I've

74

decided that I want to learn. Do you think you could teach me?"

Jack looked at her and asked, "Did something happen up at the cabin?"

Darcy didn't want to worry her friend. "No," she said shaking her head. "I just think I'd feel better, but maybe we could keep this just between us? I don't want Colin giving me or you a hard time."

Jack looked away. "I don't worry about Colin. He won't bother me none."

Before Darcy could ask Jack what he meant he said, "You'd best go on and get what you need. You don't need an old man like me keeping you."

Darcy reached out and hugged him. "You're not an old man, you're my friend. I love the time we spend together." Darcy looked back at Jack and he smiled.

"Go on and get now," he said. "How about I meet you at the diner tomorrow morning and we'll head out to your cabin to start learning to shoot."

Darcy shook her head. "Colin is patrolling past my house more. Can we go to your place instead?"

Jack took note of what Darcy said and decided he'd get to the bottom of what was going on tomorrow. "Sure," said Jack. "I'll meet you here for breakfast around eight?"

"I'll see you then." Darcy looked back at the dog and asked, "Can I bring Rebel?"

Jack nodded. "Yeah, bring him along. I'm sure he's not unfamiliar with gunshots."

Darcy walked into the general store and saw Sally at the counter. "Hi, Sally," she said with a smile.

"Hi, Darcy. It's good to see you again. Is there anything I can help you with?"

Darcy grinned like the cat who ate the canary. "I need dog supplies."

Sally smiled and asked excitedly, "You've got a dog?"

"Yep," Darcy answered proudly. "He's out in the car. Would you like to see him?"

Sally came out from around the counter. "Of course, I do. Go on out there and get him."

Darcy looked at Sally confused. "You want me to bring him in here? Isn't that against some law or code or something?"

Sally laughed. "You're ridiculous. This is my business and I say who can come in or not. Bring that dog in here. Lord knows he's probably better behaved than some people who walk in here." Darcy looked like an excited schoolgirl as she quickly walked out the door and came back with Rebel. "He's gorgeous," Sally declared. Darcy could swear that she just heard Rebel groan. She giggled and said, "I think he'd prefer handsome."

Sally brought her hand up to let Rebel smell it. "He's a great dog," she commented.

"I agree," Darcy remarked proudly. "Where can I find some dog items for this big lug? I've never had a dog before, and I could really use your help."

Sally smiled. This was a different Darcy than the one who walked into her store a few weeks ago. "You're going to need two dishes, one for water and one for food." She started leading Darcy down one of the aisles and helped her pick out everything she needed.

"Thanks, Sally. I really appreciate all of your help," she said as she held a huge bag of food in one arm and Rebel's leash in her other hand. She walked back to her car and drove back to the cabin.

Once Darcy reached the cabin, she opened the car door and was about to step out when she heard Rebel start to growl. He jumped into the front seat and pushed past her out the door. At first, she was ready to yell at him, then she caught sight of her front door. There were huge gashes throughout the exterior of the door and an axe buried in the middle of the door holding a note that said: 'Get Out!' Darcy reached for her cell to dial 911 but groaned when she remembered she had no cell service and there was no way she was going into the cabin alone. She called for Rebel and then put her car in drive and headed back to town to find Colin. This time there was no denying that someone was threatening her.

She pulled up in front of the police station and shakily ran inside. "Colin!" she yelled.

He stood up at the sound of her voice and walked towards the front of the small building. "What's wrong, Darcy?"

She gulped in some air. "Someone was at the cabin and this time they left an axe buried in my front door."

Colin grabbed his hat and started walking past her towards the door. She followed behind him and ran back to her car to follow him. "Stay here!" he ordered. Darcy didn't listen and instead they both raced out of town back up to the cabin. Rebel was sitting up in the back seat looking ready to leap out the door any second.

Colin stomped towards Darcy's car in disbelief. "You do realize you were speeding, right? I should give you a ticket."

"Are you kidding me?" Darcy argued indignantly.

"I'm not kidding. You can't go racing through town like that."

Darcy put her hand on her hip. "I was just following you. This is an emergency."

Colin shook his head. "It's not like anyone is hurt. It's just some vandalism."

"Just some vandalism? *There is an axe buried in my front door!*"

Colin walked toward Darcy's car and opened the back door to let Rebel out.

"What are you doing?" Darcy demanded.

Colin didn't look her way. "Making sure the perpetrator isn't still here."

Darcy tried to stop the dog. "I don't want Rebel hurt! Leave him in the car!"

Colin yelled back, "He's a trained dog. He knows what to do!" Before Darcy could say another word, Colin jerked opened the door and Rebel was out of the car like a shot. He ran straight towards the door and started sniffing. "Stay in the car, Darcy!" Colin ordered as he ran off, following the dog. Darcy muttered under her breath and took out her keys to unlock the door.

She knew better than to touch any evidence, so she left the axe where it was. She let herself in and looked cautiously around the house. She walked towards the kitchen to grab her kitchen knife for protection. As she walked past the table she screamed. The contract from Weston Enterprises was being held in place on the wall with a knife holding it there.

Colin came running, holding his gun in front of him. "Police!" he shouted as he scanned the room. "What happened?" he demanded. Darcy shook uncontrollably as she pointed to the knife. Colin studied the knife but didn't touch anything. He walked over to the phone and called the station for backup. Darcy sat down in a chair at the table.

Rebel was sniffing throughout the house with Colin following him. Colin had his phone out taking pictures. He shouted to Darcy as he continued investigating. "I don't think you should stay here tonight. It's not safe."

Darcy looked up in defiance. "Where am I supposed to go? I'm not letting them bully me out of my own home."

Colin's face reddened. "You can't be serious. There's an axe in your front door and a knife sticking out of your wall. This is a serious message, Darcy."

"Do you think I don't know that? If I leave now then they win. They'll know that intimidating me is working. I won't let them get away with this. I'm a big girl and I have Rebel here to protect me. I will be fine." Darcy remarked stubbornly.

Colin wanted to throw her in his car and make her listen to reason. *Why does she have to be so infuriating!* He let out a long breath trying to remain calm and said, "Well, I guess I'll just have to stay here with you then."

Darcy stood up. "That won't be necessary. I'll be fine."

Colin wanted to shake her until she listened to reason but he knew it wouldn't make a difference. She was one stubborn woman. "Have it your way then." He looked around and said, "Remember to lock the doors when I leave."

Darcy looked at him stubbornly. "I will and don't worry. I'll be fine. Thanks for your help."

Colin nodded and walked out the door. He waited on the porch until he heard the lock click and then walked out to his car. The air was getting cooler at night. He zipped up his jacket and then settled down in his car. It was going to be a long night.

Darcy sat on the couch petting Rebel, trying to calm down. That man always got her so riled up. She tried to think of who could possibly be responsible for scaring her and could only come up with Adam. He and Colin were the only two who knew about the offer. She walked back over to the contract. Maybe she should just sign the papers and go back to her life in Seattle. She wouldn't have to worry about threatening messages and there would be no Colin trying to boss her around. It would be a win-win for her.

She walked back to the bedroom and turned on the light. Rebel followed her and laid at her feet as she sat on the bed sifting through the stack of papers from the dresser drawer. There was an old picture of her grandfather and Jack standing next to each other, smiling, in their uniforms. It was an article about how both men had been deployed to Vietnam and had both returned home. It went on to describe their close friendship before and after the war.

Rebel stood up, startling Darcy out of her concentration. She stood up and stretched then followed him to the front door. She grabbed a knife, even though Rebel wasn't growling and opened the door. She was surprised to see Colin hunched up in his car outside of the cabin. *You have got to be kidding me. That man is so frustrating!* She marched out of the cabin and banged on his window. He jumped with a start. "What are you doing out here?" she demanded.

Colin rolled down his window and said, "If you're not going to town then I'll keep watch out here. It's my job to keep the citizens of West Forks safe."

Darcy crossed her arms tightly in front of her. "It's freezing out here!"

"I'll be fine," Colin remarked. "What are you doing outside anyway?"

Darcy pointed her head towards Rebel. "The dog needed to go out."

Colin looked towards Rebel trotting up to them. "Well, he looks ready to go inside. I suggest you do the same."

Darcy had that fiery look in her eye again. "I'll go in when I'm ready."

Colin sighed and said, "Suit yourself. It's a little cold out here so I'm going to roll up my window now. Goodnight, Darcy." Colin rolled up the window and turned his shoulders so that he wasn't facing her. He smiled to himself as he heard her grumble in frustration then turned and watched her stomp back towards the cabin. Rebel stood uncertainly between the cabin and the police car.

Darcy turned and said, "Come on, Rebel, let's go in." She looked at Colin huddled up in his car. "Come on, Colin, you might as well come in too. It's too cold to be staying out here."

Colin smiled at Rebel and walked next to the dog towards the cabin. He stood inside the door as Darcy stormed off and came back with pillows and blankets. "You can stay on the couch but in the morning, you're leaving, deal?"

Colin looked around and replied, "I can't make any promises until I catch whoever is doing this."

Darcy rolled her eyes and turned around. "Come on, Rebel, you're coming to bed with me." Colin admired Darcy's backside as she walked towards the bedroom. He shook his head, *Lucky dog.*

Darcy climbed into bed as Rebel stood next to her bed looking at her pathetically. "Lay down," she ordered. He slowly lay down next to the bed and looked sadly up at her. Darcy's heart melted. "Fine," she said. "I guess there's room up here for you too. Just don't hog the bed."

Chapter 8

The next morning Darcy woke up and looked at the dog lying at her feet. She smiled and climbed out of bed. Rebel stretched and hopped down beside her. Darcy padded into the kitchen then frowned when she remembered Colin sleeping on her couch. She turned up the music on her cell phone to maximum volume and began to brew a pot of coffee. She was supposed to meet Jack for breakfast at eight and didn't want anything or anyone to make her late. Colin, startled awake, sat up and rubbed his face. He looked over at Darcy and then stood up to stretch all the kinks out of his body.

Darcy looked over. "Would you like a cup of coffee?"

Colin smiled. "If it's not too much trouble." Darcy took down another mug and poured Colin a cup. He walked towards her. "Thanks." He took a sip and his head followed Rebel as the dog walked to the door and stood patiently. "I'll let him out," Colin offered. Darcy nodded and then walked over to the couch to start folding up the blankets. Colin looked over at Darcy. "Thank you for letting me stay here last night. I know you're not happy about it, but until we find out who is doing this you need to be careful."

Darcy nodded in agreement. "I don't want to seem rude, but I have a date for breakfast at Frank's Diner at eight and I really don't want to be late." Colin lifted his eyes in surprise but didn't say anything. He cleared his throat and placed his mug in the sink. "I have to get going anyway." He picked up his hat and placed it on his head. He grabbed his jacket and opened the door. Rebel came trotting back in and walked towards his food dish. "See you around, Darcy."

Darcy finished getting dressed and then grabbed Rebel's leash. She clicked the leash onto his collar and locked the door behind her. The dog jumped into the back of the car and Darcy climbed in and started it. She arrived at Frank's Diner exactly at eight and saw Jack waiting for her. "I was wondering if you changed your mind," commented Jack.

Darcy took off her jacket and said, "Not a chance. Colin slept at the cabin last night and I had to get rid of him before I could leave."

Jack gave a sly grin. "So, you and Colin huh?"

Darcy took a sip of coffee. "What? No! Never! I came home to find an axe deeply embedded in my door, so I ran to get Colin because it seemed like the right thing to do and he came out to investigate. He insisted that I not stay there. I insisted on not leaving and in the end, he looked so uncomfortable and cold in his car that I told him to sleep on the couch. This morning he left. That's it!"

Jack threw money on the table and started to stand up. "What you do is your business, Darcy. I ain't the kind to judge. Let's get back to you telling me about this axe in your door." Darcy walked behind Jack as they left the diner. She followed him out of town to a little white house at the dead end of a dirt road. When they had finally stopped Darcy let Rebel out of the car and didn't bother to put on his leash. He sniffed around while Darcy followed Jack into the little house. Darcy was surprised to see the house was neat and tidy, something she didn't expect from an old bachelor.

She stood in the kitchen looking out a window facing an empty field. Jack left the room and then came back in carrying a rifle. Darcy stared at it and immediately felt sick to her stomach.

Jack however seemed very relaxed. He smiled and said, "Let's walk out back and have us some fun."

Darcy didn't smile back and said, "Somehow I doubt this will be fun, Jack. I'm here strictly to learn how to protect myself and I doubt I'll even use it." She followed him out into the field with Rebel trotting behind.

He laid the rifle on the picnic table. "First thing you need to learn is safety. This is a weapon, not a toy."

Darcy looked at him and replied sarcastically, "I know that, Jack."

Jack ignored her. "The next thing to remember is not to assume anything." Darcy blushed as Jack looked pointedly at her. He pointed out the different parts of the gun. He explained how to use the safety and then showed her how to properly hold the rifle. "Okay, now look through the scope at the target. You should put the target right in the center of the cross-hairs." He waited for Darcy to line things up. "When you have lined up your target then click off the safety." He watched Darcy get ready and then he said, "When you feel ready, lean forward a little so that the kick of the gun won't knock you off balance, then aim and pull the trigger."

Darcy took her time and then fired. She hit the outer part of the target.

"Not bad for your first time," commented Jack. He came over and helped Darcy reload and then gave her some pointers. She slowly began to improve and relax. Jack told her stories about her grandparents which made her laugh. She wished once again that she had been able to meet them. It was sad to think that she had been deprived of such a huge part of her life. She was grateful for the letters she'd found that helped her fill in some of the holes in her history.

***

Darcy arrived home feeling safer than she had in weeks. Rebel started whining ready to be let out. He ran towards the cabin and then stopped in front of the porch and immediately started barking and growling. Darcy looked in his direction and was startled to see a tall, lanky, dark headed man standing up from the chair that he was sitting on. "Can I help you?" Darcy asked.

The man smiled. "Darcy, you are just as pretty as your mama."

Darcy looked at Rebel standing stiffly next to her, giving a low rumbling growl. The hairs on her arm stood up. She was glad Rebel was at her side. "How did you know my mother?" she asked. She tried not to look apprehensive as she walked up onto the porch and sat down in a chair that had a stick lying next to it, thanks to Rebel. She knew she would use it as a weapon if this man meant her any harm. Darcy motioned to a seat farthest from her and he sat down.

"We were married. I'm your daddy, sweetheart. I've come home."

Darcy stared dumbfounded. He leaned toward her and Rebel lifted his head, growled, and bared his teeth. Darcy knew if he moved any closer that Rebel would pounce. The man sat back nonchalantly and looked at her with self-satisfaction. Darcy cleared her throat trying to process what she'd just been told. "You're my father?" she asked still in disbelief.

"In the flesh," he said spreading his hands.

Darcy grew uneasy and could feel Rebel's tension. "I thought you were in jail," she whispered.

The man laughed. "I was but I've been out for years. I tried to find you, but your mama kept moving around, making that impossible. I figured that once your mama passed on, you'd eventually end up here."

Where was Colin when she needed him? Darcy looked at him guardedly. "What do you want, Tommy?"

Tommy looked at her. "All I want is to get to know you. We're family." He scratched his head and continued, "in fact, if I remember correctly, we're the only family we've got."

Darcy thought of her daughter. *No, we're not, but you'll never know that.*

Tommy stood up and so did Rebel. Darcy stood up ready to protect herself. Tommy kept the appearance of looking relaxed. He looked from Rebel to Darcy, "I'll be in town for a few days if you'd like to talk. I may have made some mistakes in the past, but I'm rehabilitated now. I just wanted to make up for lost time and maybe with a little luck have a relationship with my only daughter." He stepped off the porch and started walking down the road. Darcy thought about following him but changed her mind. She and Rebel went inside. She walked through the cabin and double checked that all the windows and doors had remained locked.

Darcy picked up the phone to call Colin but then put it down. She wasn't helpless and what would she say anyway? My dad showed up on my doorstep. There was no crime in that. In fact, she grudgingly admitted, he appeared to be sincere. She walked back into the bedroom and pulled out the private investigator's file. She sifted through the papers, trying to find out more about Tommy. There had to be something she missed but it was futile. All of the investigator's information revolved around her and her mother. She mumbled in frustration. She wished she had internet service to investigate his past a little further. She'd find Jack in the morning and get his take on it.

Until then, she'd start a fire in the fireplace, pour herself a glass of wine, and curl up on the couch with her book. She'd never started a fire before, thanks to her gas fireplace in her apartment. *How hard could it be?* She stooped down and picked up some of the small sticks that she had gathered from the yard and piled them in the fireplace to use for kindling. Then she rolled up bits of paper and stuck them between the sticks. She grabbed a lighter out of the kitchen drawer and walked back. She clicked the lighter and a flame flickered. She lit the edge of one of the papers and watched as the flame slowly crept up the edge and began to glow brighter. She watched as the other papers began to catch the flame and slowly the kindling began to burn. She placed a few logs on top and stood back to admire her work. *Not bad*, she thought with satisfaction.

She walked into the kitchen, poured herself a glass of wine and grabbed her book before plopping down on the couch. Rebel loped over and curled up on the floor next to her. She read while the fire blazed higher and she could feel the chill in the cabin start to subside. She'd only read a few pages before she heard Rebel snoring. She smiled despite herself. She closed her book and then her eyes. She drifted off to sleep relishing in the comfort of a warm fire and a loyal dog by her side.

She jumped at the sound of Rebel barking excitedly. She looked around her and noticed that the cabin was filling up with smoke. She quickly grabbed the phone and dialed 911.

Colin answered on the first ring. "West Forks Police Department, what is your emergency?"

Darcy yelled into the phone. "Colin, its Darcy! My cabins on fire! Hurry!" She hung up and ran into the kitchen. She had once read that flour could put out a fire or was it salt? She couldn't remember so she grabbed both and began to pour the contents onto the fire which thankfully was still contained in the fireplace. She had to smother it somehow.

Luckily, the logs she had placed in there hadn't completely caught fire. She opened her door and grabbed her oven mitts. She shoved them on her hands, grabbed one of the logs then she raced to the door and threw it out into the yard. The log had burned a hole in the mitt, but she didn't care. She ran back to the fire and grabbed the second log and did the same thing. Now she only had the kindling to contend with. She raced to the sink and began filling anything she could find with water and threw it on the fire. The fire appeared to finally be out, but the cabin was filled with smoke. Rebel was barking frantically as she called to him and they both ran outside.

As she gulped in the fresh air, her lungs burned and tears trailed down her face from the sting of the smoke. She started shaking uncontrollably and sat down in one of the chairs on the porch. Rebel whined next to her and placed his head on her lap. She first saw Colin then fire trucks roaring up to the cabin. The firemen were pulling out their hoses and the fire chief was running towards the house.

Colin reached her first. "Are you all right?"

She couldn't speak and immediately started hyperventilating. Colin down sat next to her, putting his arms around her and ordering her to take deep breaths. He was grateful that for once she listened.

Sometime later, the fire chief walked out of the house towards Colin and Darcy. "Looks like you put it out, Darcy. We'll let the smoke clear and investigate more tomorrow. It looks like it started in the chimney. Did you clean the chimney out before you lit that fire?" Darcy shook her head no. "It's something that should always be done, especially when a building has been sitting empty for a few years. Birds make nests in abandoned chimneys as well as other critters."

Colin looked at Darcy. "Why don't you stay with me tonight? You can't stay here anyway until the investigation is over." Darcy looked at him gratefully. Colin smiled. "I owe you one and I promise that I'll be on my best behavior."

Darcy replied, "As long as I can take the couch. I don't want to put you out."

Colin opened his mouth to protest but noted the look in Darcy's eyes. "Fine."

She stood up exhausted and called to Rebel. The three of them walked towards the police car. "Do I have to sit in the back?" Darcy asked jokingly.

Colin smiled. "Actually, yes, it's protocol."

Darcy stopped at the car. "You've got to be kidding."

Colin laughed. "Yes, I'm kidding. Climb up front and Rebel can sit in the back."

She sat in the front seat and started to shiver, the magnitude of the night catching up with her.

"Are you cold?" Colin asked, adjusting the temperature in the car.

"No, it's just nerves. I can't believe I almost burned down the cabin. How stupid could I be?" she said angrily.

Colin started the car and slowly began to drive forward. "It's an easy mistake when you're not used to having a fireplace. I'm just glad that you weren't hurt."

Colin pulled into the station and parked the car.

"Are you still working?" Darcy asked.

"No, but I'd like to drive my own vehicle home." He pointed to a two-door forest green jeep with a black soft top and a black winch attached to the front. He had all terrain tires and not a speck of dust on the body.

Darcy raised an eyebrow at him. "I would never have expected you to drive a jeep."

Colin looked at her speculatively. "What would you expect me to drive?"

She smiled. "Something much more conservative like a black or silver sedan."

Colin put a hand over his heart, looking wounded. "Ouch that hurt." They laughed as Colin opened the door and said, "Come on, let's go home. It's been a long day." He walked over to open Darcy's door, but she beat him to it so instead he let Rebel out of the back.

They walked over to the jeep and climbed in. Darcy smiled. "Colin, you are full of surprises. I never figured you for a stick shift sort of guy."

Colin grinned. "There's a lot you don't know about me, Darcy." He started the jeep, revved the engine, and spun out of the parking lot, leaving a black streak in their wake.

Chapter 9

Colin's house was only ten minutes from the station, and they rode there in silence. Darcy took in the modest little farmhouse and was surprised to see how well it was kept up. She got out of the jeep and Rebel stood beside her. She took in the white wraparound porch, adorned with a porch swing and two red rockers. A red tin roof sat atop the rest of the white house. It wasn't what she pictured for a bachelor. "Are you married, or do you live with your mother?" Darcy asked.

Colin looked perplexed. "Neither why would you ask me that?"

Darcy shrugged. "This just wasn't the bachelor pad I envisioned you living in."

Colin lifted an eyebrow. "Are you disappointed?"

Darcy shook her head and tried to regroup. "No, just pleasantly surprised."

"Oh, I understand," Colin replied as he walked toward the house.

"Understand what?" Darcy asked.

Colin kept walking. "Oh nothing."

Darcy kept up with his pace. "What was it you were going to say?"

Colin stopped and looked at her. "You'll take it the wrong way. Let's just forget it."

Darcy wasn't about let the matter drop. "Go ahead, Colin, tell me."

Colin shrugged. "I was going to say that I forgot that you were one of those high maintenance city girls who always judge a book by its cover."

Darcy stopped walking. "*What!* I can't believe you just said that. You hardly even know me!"

Colin shrugged and began walking up the steps to the house. "I'm just calling it like I see it. Don't get so bent out of shape. You were raised as a city girl. It's understandable that you would be high maintenance. It's in your DNA."

Darcy was livid. "*In my DNA!* You are incorrigible! C'mon, Rebel, we're leaving." She turned around and started stalking off until she realized she didn't have her car. She refused to ask Colin for a ride, so she just kept walking towards the edge of the yard. She stopped when she realized that Rebel wasn't beside her. She turned around and saw him sitting next to Colin who was standing on the porch. *Traitor,* she thought.

She turned around and continued to walk. Colin called after her, "Just remember that when you encounter a wild animal do not show fear and do not run away. You probably don't want to engage in physical contact either." He laughed.

Darcy squared her shoulders and began walking. She tried to ignore the fact that it was getting dark and she didn't even have a flashlight. She would be damned if she went back to Colin's house. She walked along the road and saw a light shining through the window of a barn. She walked towards the barn and slid open the door. She inhaled the smell of fresh hay as she stepped inside and immediately began to feel warmer. She heard a snort and walked towards one of the stalls. A beautiful brown and white pinto horse stood majestically, looking at her. She slowly walked towards it and put up her hand. The horse sniffed her hand and she gently moved her hand to pet alongside of its face.

She heard whinnies coming from another stall and walked towards the sound. Standing on fresh hay was another pinto that could have been a twin to the first one. Darcy eyed a bucket of apples sitting next to the barn door. She walked over and grabbed two of them. She fed one to the first horse and then the second apple to the other. She jumped at the sound of a deep voice behind her.

"You know, it's courteous to ask before you feed the horses."

Darcy turned to face Colin. "Have you been following me?" she accused.

Colin shook his head. "It's not all about you, Darcy. You're free to come and go as you like. I just came out to feed my horses."

"These are yours?" she asked in surprise.

Colin let out an exasperated breath. "Yes. Why does everything about me surprise you?"

Darcy looked chagrined. "I'm sorry. I appreciate all of your help, I really do. Can we please just start over?"

Colin smiled and slowly walked over to Darcy and held out his hand. "I'm Colin, I'm the sheriff of West Falls and this is my home."

Darcy smiled and held out her hand. "It's nice to meet you, Colin. I'm Darcy and you have a very lovely home. Your horses are beautiful too." They shook hands and Darcy felt an electric jolt run through her. Her pulse quickened at the attraction she felt for this man.

Colin was slow to pull away. "Would you like to help me feed the horses and then go up to the house for a cup of coffee?"

Darcy looked from the horse to him. "Yes, I'd like that very much."

Colin walked over, scooped feed into a pail, and handed it to Darcy. "Here you go. Just dump it in his trough next to that hay bale."

Darcy did as she was instructed and handed the pail back to Colin. She walked back towards the horse and began to run her hand along its flank. "They are absolutely beautiful," she commented. "Emma would love this."

Colin looked up at her. "Who's Emma?"

Darcy smiled and kept petting the horse. "Emma is my daughter. She's away at camp for the summer while I'm here cleaning out the cabin."

Colin replied. "Now who's the one full of surprises?"

Darcy laughed. "She's pretty amazing. She's an eleven-year-old going on sixteen, but she sure loves animals."

Colin reached for a brush and handed the other to Darcy. They both started brushing the horses in companionable silence. "Does she have any pets back home?" Colin asked.

"No, our apartment doesn't allow pets."

Colin kept his eyes on the horse. "Then you'll have to bring her here one of these days."

Darcy shrugged. "I'd love to but I'm hoping to have things tied up here before camp ends." Colin opened his mouth to speak but Darcy interrupted before he asked the inevitable question. "Horses are such magnificent creatures. Do you ride much?"

Colin took her brush and put them away. "Yes, they are and yes, I enjoy going for a ride when I get home from a rough day. Do you ride?"

Darcy shook her head. "I haven't in years. I used to love it though."

Colin paused then said, "Maybe in the morning we can go for a ride before I take you home."

Darcy smiled. "I'd like that."

***

The next morning Darcy woke up to the smell of coffee brewing. Her back ached from sleeping on the couch but she had insisted. She stood up, stretched, and walked into the kitchen to get a cup. She bit her tongue when she saw Colin in front of the stove, scrambling eggs. He turned around and smiled at her. "Good morning, Darcy. Did you sleep okay?"

Darcy was sticking by her guns about the couch. "I slept perfectly fine. Your couch is quite comfortable."

Colin turned back to the stove so Darcy wouldn't see him hiding the laugh that threatened to erupt. He had fallen asleep on the couch before and it was far from comfortable. He grabbed a plate and filled it with eggs, added a couple of pieces of toast and handed it to Darcy.

"No, thank you. I'll just have a piece of toast."

Colin shook his head and carried his plate to the table. "You really should eat before we go riding. You need more than toast."

Darcy smiled and replied. "I'll be fine, really."

After breakfast they walked out to the barn and Darcy helped Colin saddle up the horses. She climbed up and grabbed the reins then turned the horse to follow Colin. It was a beautiful day. The mountains looked majestic and wildflowers popped up sporadically across the field. Colin took her along a well-traveled path winding through a shady patch of trees that led down to a stream. They climbed off the horses and led them to the water for a drink. Darcy looked up at the bright blue sky filled with cotton candy clouds floating overhead.

"It's such a gorgeous day!" Darcy said. "Thanks for taking me on a ride this morning. It's a nice way to start the day before I am thrown back into the chaos of what is my life."

Colin looked up at the sky and then squinted when he turned towards her. "I heard from the fire inspector this morning."

Darcy looked at him in surprise. "What did he say? Can I go back home now?"

Colin put up his hand to stop the barrage of questions that were about to start. "Yes, you can go back home, but I was wondering about something."

Darcy looked at him, bewildered. "What's that?"

Colin looked her straight in the eye. "It appears that there were wads of newspapers, a blanket, and some insulation stuffed in your chimney. Would you happen to know anything about that?"

Darcy looked confused. "No. No idea. Maybe the chimney was drafty since the fireplace was no longer used?"

Colin nodded. "That's a possibility, I suppose. Look, I hope you don't take this the wrong way, but I've gotta ask. Are you running away from something or... someone?"

Darcy could feel her anger starting to boil. "What are you implying?"

Colin knew he was about to have it with both barrels, but he wasn't going to back down. "What I mean is that you turn up here and stay in a cabin in the middle of nowhere. On numerous occasions someone has been breaking and entering your cabin. You had a knife holding a sales contract to your wall and let's not forget about the axe in the middle of the door. Now you nearly died in a house fire. So, I'll ask again, are you running away or hiding from someone? An abusive husband or boyfriend maybe?"

Darcy climbed back onto her horse and turned around towards the house. "Oh, for crying out loud, Colin, there's no husband, abusive or otherwise. Not that it's any of your business, but my husband died fighting in Afghanistan ten years ago. I inherited the house after my mother passed away, which I may point out, you've seen the deed to. It has been in my family for generations. I have a right to live there, and as for the axe in my door, you're the sheriff, you figure it out." She pulled on the reins and started back in the direction of the house. Every time they started to get along, he ruined it with his incessant interrogations. She couldn't wait to get away from this infuriating man.

Colin shook his head in defeat and turned his horse around to follow Darcy back to the house. They were both silent and the mood had changed from enjoyable to tense. Darcy dismounted her horse and led her into the stable. Colin followed and took off the saddle. They both brushed down the horses in silence.

Colin couldn't stand it anymore. "Darcy, I know you're irritated with me, but this is my job. For the most part, I've enjoyed getting to know you—"

Darcy interrupted. "For the most part?" and Colin could see Darcy getting riled up again.

"Damn it, Darcy, you don't even give me a chance to finish my sentence before you're jumping down my throat. Can you just listen for a change?"

Darcy crossed her arms and looked at him expectantly.

He began again. "What I was trying to say is that I don't want to see you get hurt. I don't know what's going on, but I aim to find out, and if there's something you're not telling me that could help me keep you safe, then I wish you would."

Darcy put down the brush in exasperation and said, "I swear I don't know anyone who would want to hurt me. I'm not running from anything. I'm here because I inherited the cabin. That's all."

Colin looked at her and could tell she wasn't lying. "All right then, let's get you home."

Darcy was afraid of how much damage might have been caused by the fire. She hoped it wasn't too bad and she could salvage it. She called for Rebel who came running towards her and hopped up into the jeep. Darcy closed the door and climbed in the front.

Colin pulled up in front of Darcy's house. They all climbed out of the jeep and Rebel stayed by Darcy's side. She walked up and pushed open the door. She was immediately inundated with the pungent smell of smoke. She stepped outside to catch her breath and to pull herself together. The sight of black soot covering the walls, furniture, and the ceiling was overwhelming.

Colin led her to a chair on the porch and sat down next to her. She let out a loud sigh.

"I'm sorry. I guess I'm just a little overwhelmed. I didn't expect that much damage."

Colin nodded in sympathy. "I could stick around and help, if you'd like."

Darcy smiled sadly and shook her head. "I'm sure you have better things to do with your time. I've got nothing but time. I'll do it. It was a mess the first time I cleaned it, and this will require more elbow grease, but I'll manage."

Colin stood up and walked into the house. He opened all the doors and windows to allow the cabin to air out. He walked back out onto the porch with his hands on his hips, scanning the area for any clue of what happened. He just didn't believe that anyone who stayed in that cabin would have blocked the chimney in that fashion. He trusted his gut and his gut was telling him that something wasn't right. He planned on going back to the office and going through the fire inspector's paperwork first thing.

Darcy studied Colin and noticed the determined look on his face. "It's okay if you have to leave. I'll be fine, really."

Colin didn't agree, but he knew better than to argue with her. He put on his sunglasses and grimaced. "I do have to get back to the office, but if you see anything suspicious or out of place call me."

Darcy smiled sadly. "Okay, Sheriff."

Colin took off his glasses and looked Darcy in the eye. "I'm serious, Darcy."

Darcy stood up and dusted off her jeans. Rebel stood up next to her. "I will call, I promise. I want to solve this just as badly as you do." Colin nodded and walked towards his jeep.

Darcy watched him drive off and then turned back towards the house. She took a deep breath for strength and looked at Rebel. "Well, boy, let's get started." Rebel looked at her and then cautiously took a step inside the cabin.

She filled the sink with water, vinegar, and baking soda. She dipped a cloth in the hot water and started wiping down the counters in the kitchen. She was lost in thought as she continued to scrub the walls and was startled to hear Sally calling her name through the front door. Darcy turned around and was surprised to see a group of people, all holding supplies. "What are you all doing here?" she asked, astounded.

Sally smiled. "Well, we heard about what happened and thought you could use a hand."

Darcy's eyes filled with tears. "I would love the help. Come on in." Darcy held opened the front door as person after person filed in.

Sally held up a bottle of cleaner and said, "I hope this is the type you like, I don't use the stuff myself."

Darcy laughed and said, "I don't either. I just use water, vinegar, and baking soda. Isn't that what you told me?"

Sally laughed and hugged her. "You're learning; now let's get this place back to looking as good as new."

Everyone scrubbed and cleaned while chatting and laughing. Darcy shook her head in amazement that all these people would choose to spend the day helping her. They were beginning to feel like family, and she hadn't felt that since her mom died.

Once everything was gleaming and the black soot had been removed, Darcy spoke up. "Thanks, everyone, I couldn't have done this without you. I wish I could repay you all somehow."

Sally spoke up. "Now you're being silly girl. We take care of our own out here and you're one of our own. You'd do the same if it were someone else in the community."

Frank spoke up. "Let's quit all the mushy stuff. I'm starving. Everyone head on over to my diner and grab a bite to eat. It's my treat." Some people cheered while others quickly started gathering their supplies. Frank looked at Darcy. "I expect you to be there too, missy."

Darcy grinned. "I wouldn't dare miss it, Frank. Just let me get cleaned up a little." Frank gave her a curt nod and walked out towards his truck.

After everyone had left Darcy looked down at Rebel. "Well, Rebel, looks like we found us a home. What do you think?" Rebel wagged his tail in agreement then stretched and flopped down on the porch to lie in the sun. Darcy quickly got changed and washed the soot off her face, then shut and locked the door. "C'mon boy, let's go." Rebel lazily stood up and walked to the car. Darcy put the top down and drove towards town. She walked into the diner and stopped to talk to a few people on her way to the counter.

Frank looked out the front window. "Darcy, don't you leave that dog outside. Bring him on in here."

Darcy looked shocked. "Oh, I couldn't do that. I'm sure there's some code or regulation against letting pets into a diner."

Frank shook his head. "Woman, I am the owner of said establishment and I'm telling you to bring that dog on in here."

Darcy smiled and shook her head but did as she was told. "Rebel, come." Rebel stood up, wagging his tail and jumped out of the car and walked inside the diner. He stayed by Darcy's side and laid down by her feet. Darcy was amazed at his good behavior. She ordered a tall glass of ice water while she waited for her lunch to be served.

She was chatting with Miranda when she heard, "Is that Darcy's voice I hear?"

She turned around and saw Jack sitting in his regular booth reading the paper. She got up and walked over to him with Rebel in tow. She sat across from him and said, "Hi, Jack. How are you?"

Jack grunted, but she could see that his eyes were smiling. "Better than you from what I hear," he replied laying down his newspaper and looking intently at

Darcy. "Why in tarnation would you start a fire before checking the chimney?"

Darcy groaned. "I used to live in an apartment. I didn't have to worry about fireplaces and chimneys. But, believe me, it was a lesson learned."

Jack nodded. "Are you keeping that gun near you at all times?" Darcy shook her head. "It's a rifle Jack. It's kind of hard to lug it with me everywhere I go. People will think I'm nuts and run for cover."

Jack laughed at the image. "Darcy, I heard what stopped up the chimney. I knew your grandparents and I know for a fact that they wouldn't put that stuff in the chimney." Darcy looked at Jack, afraid to hear what was coming next. "Is there anyone who would want to hurt you?" Jack asked.

Darcy shook her head adamantly. "No, no one. I told Colin the same thing. I inherited the cabin which is what brought me here. My mom passed away a few months ago and my dad..." she stopped and looked straight into Jack's eyes. "Tommy showed up at my house the other day."

Jack took a sip of coffee and pondered this new information. "So, Tommy's back in town, eh? What did he want?"

Darcy shrugged. "Nothing really, he said he wanted to get to know me and that's it."

Jack was quiet then asked, "What about that other fella you were with a few weeks ago?"

Darcy looked confused. "What fella?"

Jack leaned forward. "That tall, dark-haired, skinny guy you were eating breakfast with."

Darcy thought for a minute and said, "Adam? He wouldn't do anything like this. He's a real estate agent and wanted to know if I was interested in selling my property."

Jack grunted. "What did you say?"

Darcy replied, "I told him I decided not to sell."

Jack huffed in exasperation. "And you don't think that's a reason to get rid of you?"

Darcy rolled her eyes. "Did you see Adam? He's a complete gentleman and not a threat. When I told him, I wasn't interested that was the end of it."

Jack folded up his newspaper. "Does Colin know about this?"

Darcy groaned. "Not you too. I'm a big girl, Jack. Colin doesn't have to know my every move. This is a free country, last I checked. By the way, since when did you and our sheriff become such good friends?"

Jack huffed. "I didn't say no such thing. I just think a woman such as yourself staying alone in the middle of the woods with someone trying to kill her would want the sheriff to be privy to this information, is all."

Darcy began to relax. "I'm sorry, Jack, I didn't mean to snap. I'm just tired and I'm angry as hell that someone is trying to run me off my land."

Jack leaned towards her. "That makes two of us."

Chapter 10

Darcy drove home later, thinking about everything that Jack had said. She wasn't about to let anyone run her off her land. She may not have called this place home for long, but she'd be damned if she was going to give it up without a fight.

She pulled up in front of the house and was surprised to see Adam sitting in a rocker on her porch. She hesitated, then got out of the car with Rebel close beside her. Rebel's hair rose on his neck and he was tense, but he didn't react. "What are you doing here, Adam?" Darcy asked.

Adam stood up and put his hands on his hips. "I heard about the fire. I thought I would check on you and make sure you were okay."

Darcy shrugged. "I'm right as rain. I thought you would be back in Billings by now."

Adam walked down the steps towards Darcy. "I had a few things that kept me tied up. I should be heading back soon. How about you? I thought you would be headed back to Seattle by now."

Darcy walked past him as he followed her back to the porch. "I changed my mind. I've decided to stick around for a while."

Adam looked around. "I can see why. It's beautiful out here." He motioned to the dog. "Who's your friend?"

Darcy leaned down to pet Rebel's black and brown coat. "I got him from a friend. His name is Rebel." Adam leaned towards Rebel and Darcy heard a low rumble coming from the dog. "I don't suggest you do that," Darcy warned. "He doesn't take kindly to people he doesn't know."

Adam leaned back. "Ah, sounds like a few locals I've met in town." Darcy looked at him in surprise. Adam laughed. "Not you. Maybe the sheriff and others I've encountered since I've been here." Darcy felt a bit of satisfaction in that.

Darcy started to speak when Adam interrupted. "Darcy, would you like to have dinner?"

Darcy looked at him in surprise. "Dinner? As in a date?"

Adam nodded. "Yes, as in a date. Ever since I've met you, I can't get you off my mind. I'd really like a chance to get to know you better, if that's okay with you."

Darcy looked at him, contemplating his offer. Maybe this would give her some of the answers she'd been looking for. "Okay, I'll go to dinner with you, but on one condition."

Adam looked at her, surprised that she'd actually agreed. "What's the condition?"

Darcy replied, "Everyone in town will be hovering, so why don't we go for pizza outside of town?"

Adam smiled. "Agreed. What if I pick you up at seven?"

Darcy was about to answer when another car pulled in and her father stepped out. She turned and inwardly groaned. For someone living in the middle of nowhere, she sure had a lot of company.

Tommy walked up to the porch and smiled easily. "Hi, Darcy." Darcy remained quiet and eyed him warily. He looked over at Adam and walked towards him with an outstretched hand. "Hi, I'm Tommy, Darcy's father, and you are?"

Adam held out his hand. "The name's Adam." The two men shook hands and Tommy stood with his hands in his pockets, acting as if he stopped by to visit every day.

"Why are you here?" Darcy asked, irritated.

Tommy smiled. "I'm just stopping by to visit with my daughter."

Darcy looked at him incredulously. "You're kidding, right? You've never had a relationship with me and now you think you can just waltz in and play daddy? That's not how this works, Tommy. Just leave, now is not a good time."

Tommy looked from Darcy to Adam. "When would be a good time?"

Adam interrupted. "Darcy, we can reschedule if you'd like."

"No, Adam, we're not going to reschedule. Tommy was just leaving."

Tommy looked at Adam. "May I have a minute with my daughter?"

Adam looked at Darcy unsure of what to do. Darcy crossed her arms in front of her, ignored Tommy, and said, "I'll see you at seven?"

Adam nodded then asked, "Are you sure you want me to leave? I'll stick around if you'd like."

Tommy laughed. "Do you think I'd harm my own daughter? Son, I'm not going to do anything."

Darcy looked at Adam and smiled. "It's okay. You can leave. I know how to take care of myself. I'm not worried about Tommy and neither should you. I will see you a seven."

Adam looked at her uncertainly. He wasn't convinced she was entirely accurate when it came to Tommy but decided to leave like she had asked him to.

Darcy crossed her arms in front of her and looked at Tommy. "What do you want Tommy?"

"Damn girl, why are you so suspicious? I just want to get to know you, that's all." Darcy sat down on a rocking chair and motioned to the other one. Tommy walked up and sat down. Darcy was quiet and looked at him expectantly. Tommy cleared his throat nervously and started to speak. "I remember the first time I walked up on this porch. I was so nervous to meet your grandfather. That man was meaner than a rattlesnake." Tommy chuckled. "I was shaking in my shoes, but your momma… she was worth it. She was the prettiest girl I had ever seen. We met at school. Did she ever tell you that?" Darcy shook her head no. "Well, we did. My family had just moved here from Texas and I didn't know anyone. My family moved around a lot, so I was used to being the new kid. I didn't care about friends until I laid eyes on your momma. She smiled at me when I sat down in the desk behind her. The teacher, Mr. Dugan, asked her to show me around." Tommy smiled, thinking back to that day. "Not only was your momma pretty, she was so smart."

He looked at Darcy. "I bet you're a lot like her." He leaned forward and spoke earnestly, "Darcy, I've made mistakes. I admit that. I'm not perfect but you are the only family I've got left and I'm the only family you've got left. All I want is for us to get to know each other. That's all."

Darcy could see that he was sincere and there was a part of her that wanted to know him. He was her dad. She cleared her throat. "I'd like that. I'm not making any promises but maybe it wouldn't hurt to spend some time together."

Tommy smiled in relief and slowly stood up. "I heard you had plans tonight and I don't want to keep you. Can we meet for breakfast tomorrow?"

Darcy stood up and stretched. "I'd like that, but why don't you come here for breakfast. If we go to Frank's Diner everyone in town will be watching and listening. I'll whip something up."

Tommy nodded and smiled. "I'd like that. I'll see you tomorrow then." He walked back to his car and drove off in the direction from which he came. Darcy looked at her watch and walked inside to get ready for her date with Adam.

***

Darcy dressed in a pair of dark jeans and a red tank top, with a denim shirt thrown over. She quickly brushed through her hair, smiling as she thought ironically about how things had changed. She would never have dressed like this for a date in Seattle. In fact, she would never have dressed like this ever. But living in West Forks had changed her and she had a feeling that it was for the better. She had easily adapted to the slower pace of life and her blog was thriving. She looked down at Rebel sitting patiently by her side and leaned down to pet him. She had never owned a dog, but now she couldn't imagine her life without one.

She heard a knock on her door and walked across the living room to answer it. Adam was standing awkwardly in a gray pinstriped suit, holding a bouquet of white roses. He smiled and said, "These are for you."

Darcy returned his smile and opened the door wider to let him in. She took the flowers from him and said, "They're beautiful, thank you." She walked over to a cupboard, pulled out a vase and filled it with water. She carefully placed the flowers in the water and put them on her small kitchen table.

She eyed Adam's suit and then looked down at herself. "I thought we were just getting pizza."

He smiled and said, "We are, but I didn't have anything else to wear. I'm just here on business, remember?"

Darcy smiled. "That's right. I forgot. I'll go change, just give me a minute." Darcy hastily went back into her room and frantically opened the closet. She pushed her clothes all the way to the other side and pulled out her little black dress that was in the far back. It was the only really nice dress she had brought with her when she came to the cabin. She quickly slipped it on and put on a pair of earrings.

When Adam saw her, he smiled. "Wow! You look beautiful."

Darcy smiled. "Thank you. I guess I do clean up well." They both laughed as he opened the door to his car and closed it behind her.

Once he was seated, he said, "You'll have to give me directions." Darcy nodded in agreement as Adam started the car. As they were driving, he said, "Can I ask you something?"

Darcy looked at him. "Sure, what is it?"

Adam took a deep breath and said, "I don't want you to take this the wrong way, but don't you miss it?"

Darcy looked confused. "Miss what?"

Adam clarified. "Don't you miss the city? I mean, let's face it, everything is more convenient in the city. We don't have to drive thirty miles to go to a pizza joint that's for sure. You don't have to start fires just to stay warm. There's always something to do. So, don't you miss it?"

Darcy shrugged and looked out the car window. "I'll admit that in the beginning I did. I actually hated it here and couldn't wait to get back to Seattle. But I don't know, there's something about this place, I guess I'm not explaining it very well." Adam opened his mouth to speak but Darcy interrupted. "There it is."

Adam turned into the parking lot and turned off the car. Darcy went to open the door but Adam said, "Wait just a minute." He walked around the car and opened her door for her.

She looked up at him in surprise. "Thank you. I can't remember the last time someone has opened my door for me. I'm feeling spoiled."

Adam closed the door behind her, put his hand on the small of her back and guided her towards the restaurant. They were seated at a table with a red and white plastic checkered tablecloth along with a vase of plastic flowers. Adam leaned over and whispered, "I'm feeling a little overdressed."

Darcy giggled. "Me too."

It was quiet as they looked at the menu and tried to decide what kind of pizza to order. A waitress walked over to take their order. "Can we have two bottles of beer and a large pizza?"

The waitress asked, "What kind of pizza would you like?" Adam looked at Darcy who shrugged. "We'd like the best that you've got. Surprise us."

The waitress smiled politely and turned to leave as Darcy and Adam burst out in laughter. Darcy looked at Adam and excused herself. She walked up to the waitress and said something quietly and then walked to the restroom.

When she came back Adam asked, "Did I forget to order something?"

Darcy smiled. "No, but we look very out of place and I just couldn't help myself. I told her that you were a food critic and I convinced you that this place has the best pizza around."

Adam tried to stifle a laugh as the waitress walked up and placed two beers in front of them. She smiled widely at Adam. "If you'd like anything else, please let me know. Your pizza will be out shortly."

Adam took a drink and shook his head. "This date will go down in the books as being one of the most memorable."

Darcy looked at him and grinned. "You've got to admit that would never happen in the city. We would have blended in with the rest of the crowd."

Adam nodded. "That's true. But there's a comfort in blending in."

Darcy looked him in the eye and said, "There's also something to be said for standing out."

The pizza arrived along with a couple of more beers. Adam took a bite. "If I had the choice to blend in or stand out, I think I'd like to blend in. In my field of work, I always have to strive to be the best. I always have to be on my A-game by looking my best and making a good impression with my clients. It would be nice not to have to worry about that, you know?"

Darcy nodded. "That makes sense. That's part of the reason I like living away from the city. No one knows me here and I don't have to impress anyone. I can just be myself."

Adam leaned back. "Hypothetically, if you could be anywhere or do anything what would you do?"

Darcy thought for a minute and then said, "I'm really not sure. I love blogging and I'm already my own boss, so I don't think I'd change my career. Maybe I'd travel more. What about you?"

Adam shrugged and said, "Quit my job and travel the world. There's too much to see and too little time to see it." The waitress brought two plates of dessert. Adam looked up in surprise. "Excuse me but we didn't order dessert."

The waitress smiled. "It's on the house," she replied, then she turned and walked away.

"Cheesecake, my favorite," Darcy giggled.

Adam continued his conversation. "Darcy, what would you do with one-point-three million dollars?"

Darcy looked up at him and tried not to look surprised. "I don't know. I'd never thought about it before you showed up on my doorstep." She knew if she wanted answers now was the time to ask. "Why does Weston Enterprises want my land so badly? I've heard they've been after it for years."

Adam was caught off guard, Darcy noted. He replied, "It's like I was telling you before. You have a lot of acreage and a beautiful lake. The ways to develop that land are endless. Why do you ask? Are you reconsidering?"

Darcy ignored the question. "I bet you would have made a significant commission off of the sale." Darcy tried to look nonchalant as she took another bite of cheesecake.

Adam cleared his throat and placed his napkin on the table. "I'm not going to disagree with you. The commission from the sale would have been nice but I have other sales in the works though so I'm not worried. I'll be honest with you. Passing up one-point-three million dollars to live in the middle of nowhere seems crazy to me." He reached over and took Darcy's hand and caressed it. "Aren't you even the least bit tempted? Just think of the life you could have. This doesn't have to be a hypothetical question, Darcy. You could have the life you dream of. Travel to Paris, vacation in the Tahiti, go anywhere and do anything you like. Why hold on to a plot of land that you knew nothing about until recently? Why live in the middle of the woods where there's nothing to do?"

Darcy trailed her finger up his arm and replied sweetly, "When you put it like that. I guess it does sound crazy."

Adam leaned in and said, "Do you want to know something crazier?" Darcy kept her gaze on her finger so that she wouldn't give anything away.

"What's that?" she asked innocently.

Adam laughed and replied, "Weston Enterprises just upped the ante. They are now prepared to offer you two-point-six million dollars."

Darcy was speechless and her hand stilled. "They doubled the offer?"

Adam smiled satisfactorily. "Yes, they doubled the offer. Was this your plan all along?"

Darcy was stunned. "No, it wasn't my plan all along. Wow, I don't know what to say."

Adam reached into his flap pocket and pulled out the contract for the sale of the property. "All you have to do is sign and the money will be yours."

Darcy smiled sweetly and took the contract from him. "Adam, this was your plan all along, wasn't it?"

He recovered well from the question. "I don't know what you mean."

She stopped smiling, "What I mean is that this was not a date but instead another sales pitch. I'd like to go home now." She stood up and slid her sweater over her shoulders.

Adam sighed. "Darcy, you're wrong. This is a date and not a sales pitch. I really like you and I do want to get to know you better. I just thought that it was important that you know what you're about to give up. Darcy," he said leaning across the table, "you could be a millionaire." She looked down at the papers in her hand. She was shaking with rage. She ripped them up and threw them at him. "I believe we're done here. I'll find my own way home." She stood up and started walking out the door as Adam hurriedly threw money on the table and followed her out. "Darcy, wait!"

She stood rigidly wishing he'd just go away. He walked up to her. "I'm not just going to abandon you in this god forsaken place. Get in the car. I'll drive you home." He reached for the door handle, but Darcy was quicker. She yanked open the door and said, "I am fully capable of opening my own door. Please just take me home." Adam climbed into the driver's seat and they rode back to Darcy's cabin in silence. He turned off the car and got out to open the door.

Darcy looked at him angrily. "There's no need to walk me to the door. I'll be fine." Adam opened his mouth to speak but she interrupted before he had the chance. "Adam, don't. My mind is made up and the answer is still *no*." She slammed the door and hurriedly walked up the porch to let herself in.

Once the door was closed and Adam knew she was safe, he slowly drove off. "Damn!" he yelled, as he hit the steering wheel.

Chapter 11

Bang! Darcy jumped up out of bed and went running out into the living room. The front door was wide open, and she heard an ominous growl coming from outside. "Rebel!" She ran outside and saw Rebel's fur standing on end and heard a low menacing growl coming from the mouth that was wrapped around the neck of a man lying on the porch floor.

"Darcy," the man croaked. "Call off your dog."

Darcy looked down in shock. "Tommy! Why are you here so early and what did you do to my dog?"

"If you call off your dog, I'll tell you."

Darcy leaned against the door jam and crossed her arms in front of her. "I think I'll let you explain first and then I'll call off my dog."

Tommy could barely breathe and said, "I came for breakfast. Remember, you invited me? We never set a time but apparently, I'm a little early. I was sitting on your porch step, wondering if I should wake you or not, when I saw something lying in front of your door and I wanted to get a closer look. When I stepped up onto the porch there was a decapitated bird lying on the porch in front of your door and I got worried about you. I kicked the bird out of the way and tried the door. It was unlocked so I opened it in case you needed help and your dog attacked me."

Darcy rolled her eyes and sighed, "Rebel, stand down." Rebel let go but sat next to Tommy watching him. Tommy could tell that one wrong move and Rebel was ready to lunge at him again, and maybe this time he wouldn't be so lucky.

Tommy looked at the dog, then at Darcy. "Seriously, Darcy! You're acting like I'm a criminal or something."

Darcy eyed him. "Aren't you?"

Tommy blew out a long breath and muttered, "Former criminal. I've changed but if that's what you want to believe about me, fine. I'll leave right now and never bother you again. Just call off your dog so I can get up."

Darcy was quietly contemplating what to do then shook her head in disbelief and relented. She looked at him and then at Rebel. "Rebel, come." The dog obediently stood up and walked over to sit beside Darcy, but he kept his eyes on Tommy who stood up and dusted off his clothes. He looked at Darcy and then turned around to leave.

He was halfway across the yard when Darcy yelled, "Tommy, stop! Don't leave!"

He stopped and hung his head then turned around and looked at Darcy in defeat. "Are you sure?" he asked.

Darcy stepped onto the porch. "Yes, I'm sure."

Tommy turned around and walked back towards the cabin.

"Come in and I'll put on some coffee," Darcy muttered. Tommy stepped through the door and she closed it behind them.

"Wow," remarked Tommy. "This is like taking a step back in time." He sat at the table looking around as Darcy carried over two coffee mugs. They were silent for a moment before he said, "I'm sorry if it seemed like I was breaking in. I was worried, that's all."

Darcy looked at him. "Worried about what?"

"Worried about you, that's what. I came over to see you just like we had agreed on yesterday and I see a decapitated bird on your porch along with the word 'MOVE' written in blood."

Darcy stood up. "What? You didn't say anything about words written in blood!" She ran to the door and saw the raven lying dead, with its head disconnected from his body. She covered her mouth with her hand when she saw the word 'MOVE' written in blood on the wall of the cabin. She stomped off in anger and walked inside to grab a broom.

"What are you doing?" Tommy asked.

Darcy looked up at him incredulously. "What does it look like I'm doing? I'm getting that bird off my porch."

"Don't!" Tommy exclaimed as he grabbed her arm to stop her. "Somebody's obviously giving you a message. Do you have any idea who could have done this?"

Darcy put down the broom and shook her head no. "What should we do?" Darcy asked.

Tommy shrugged and sat down next to her. "I can't believe I'm saying this, but I think you should call the police."

Darcy groaned and then replied, "I guess you're right. Colin will love this one." She picked up her phone and dialed Colin then sat down on her rocker next to Tommy and waited.

"So, Darcy," Tommy said awkwardly. "Tell me about yourself."

Darcy looked at him in disbelief and replied sarcastically, "Well, I've just discovered that I have a father, someone wants me gone, and I have no one to turn to except my dog who can't really give me any advice."

Tommy looked at the German Shepherd sitting at Darcy's side. "Well, at least he'll keep you safe, that's a plus. Look, I'm not quite sure what you've heard about me but I'm here and I'm trying. I made a mistake and I've learned my lesson. I'd like to make things right between us."

Darcy eyed him warily but nodded. "Okay, Tommy. If that's true, then tell me why you're really here."

Tommy looked at her uncomfortably and cleared his throat. He leaned forward and folded his hands together. "I knew your mama wouldn't let me be anywhere near you and to be honest I can't say I blame her. For a while I was drinking heavily and at times abusive. I'm not proud of that. I really screwed up. Your mama was a proud woman and refused to forgive me, and even if she did, her daddy wasn't one to forgive and forget. I did my time and paid my debt to society. I started going to AA. I got a job as a mechanic and I worked hard. Once I heard your mama had passed, I knew you would inherit the cabin."

Darcy listened and really wanted to believe him, but her gut wasn't that trusting. "Well, you found me, now what?"

Tommy looked at her confused. "What do you mean? I want to get to know you. Maybe we could be friends or maybe eventually you can let me back into your life as your father."

Darcy's eyes welled up and she sighed heavily. Before she could say anything else, Colin pulled up in his cruiser. He climbed out of the car and walked briskly across the yard. He eyed Tommy in surprise. "Tommy, I didn't know you were in town."

Tommy locked eyes with Colin, but didn't smile. "I haven't been in town long and I'm no longer on probation, so I didn't see the need to check in with the local sheriff."

Colin looked over at Darcy and asked. "Are you all right?" Darcy nodded, "I'm okay, but I can't say the same about the bird lying on my porch."

Colin stepped up onto the porch and walked over to the bird. He leaned over studying it and then looked at the message written in blood.

He took a picture of the word 'MOVE', then of the raven. He slid a pair of plastic gloves over his hands and picked up the dead bird and placed it in a plastic bag. "I doubt we'll find any evidence on the bird, but we'll try." Colin looked back at Tommy and said, "Where were you when this bird met his demise?"

Tommy shook his head. "Give it a rest, Sheriff. I'm the one who told her to call you."

Colin looked back at Darcy and asked, "How do you know this man?"

Darcy rolled her eyes and crossed her arms in front of her. "I'm surprised you don't already know the answer to that, Sheriff. I believe you once told me you know everything that goes on in your town."

Colin shrugged and turned to leave. "I suggest you be more careful in the company you keep," he said.

Darcy marched across the yard towards him. "Colin, he didn't do it. I can vouch for him."

Colin eyed Tommy sitting on the porch watching them. "How do you know, Darcy? He could have killed that bird and then told you to call me."

Darcy looked away and then back at him. "I doubt that. He's my father."

Colin stared at her dumbfounded. "You've got to be kidding."

Darcy shook her head. "I wish I was. He wants us to get to know each other and let's face it, he's the only family I've got left."

Colin let out a long breath. "Well, they say you can pick your friends but not your family. Just be careful, Darcy. I don't trust him."

Darcy looked back at Tommy, smiled, and then turned back towards Colin. "Don't worry; I can take care of myself. I don't trust him either, but I know he wasn't responsible for this."

Colin climbed back in his jeep. "I'll let you know what I find out, but trust no one. All these incidents are not random. Someone wants you gone."

Darcy let out a long breath. "I know, and I'll be careful. Let me know if you find out anything."

Colin drove away.

Darcy turned around, walked back to the porch and sat in the rocking chair across from Tommy. He looked at her sympathetically. "I didn't come here to cause trouble for you, Darcy. I hope you believe that."

Darcy nodded. Tommy cleared his throat and said, "Would you like me to leave? We can talk another time."

Darcy looked at him skeptically and then said, "No, this time is as good as any, but before you start, I have a few questions for you."

Tommy groaned. "Save your breath. I could tell you are a lot like your momma. I went to jail for assault and battery. Yes, I hit your mom. I'm not proud of it and it's a regret that I'll have to live with for the rest of my life. I made a mistake and I have a lot of regrets, but that one was the worst. Your momma packed you up as the cops were hauling me off and the two of you disappeared."

Darcy looked at him and said, "You left out the part where mom shot you."

Tommy looked at her in surprise. "Yes, yes she did." He smiled ruefully. "But like I said, I made mistakes and to be honest, I probably deserved it."

Darcy felt her reserve beginning to wane and she felt herself smile. "You absolutely did," she said. They both laughed. "It's getting hot out. Do you want to come in for breakfast?"

Tommy shook his head. "I've lost my appetite with all this excitement, but if you have a glass of ice-cold tea, I'll gladly take that."

Darcy stood up and walked inside to get their drinks and settled back onto the wooden rocking chair. The same one her grandmother probably sat in, and her mother after that. It appeared there was a history of remarkable women in her family.

Tommy took a long sip. "Okay, your turn. Tell me something about you."

Darcy thought for a while not sure how much she wanted to divulge. "I live in Seattle and as you know I came out here once my mom died. When I first arrived, I hated this place but I've grown to like it. Everyone has been so nice and to be honest now I'm not sure where I belong anymore." She hadn't intended bearing her soul to this stranger, but it was out there.

Tommy shook his head and laughed. "You and me both. I've been to many cities and seen some amazing sights along the way, but this place...this place has always been home. The difference between us is that you can stay if you want to but me... I'll never be able to. In this town, once you mess with one of their own, they don't forgive and believe me, they never forget."

Darcy sipped her tea. "People make mistakes. It's a fact of life."

Tommy was quiet for a moment then turned his head, gazing past the lush green grass towards the mountains that stood steadfast behind the lake. He could hear peepers that were surrounding the lake then he pushed away thoughts from a more peaceful time in his life. That's not his life any more. "Well," Tommy said, as he cleared his throat and stood up. "I'd best get going." He looked at her and smiled. "It was nice getting to know you, Darcy. Thank you for agreeing to talk with me."

Darcy looked up confused. "You will come again, won't you? Maybe next time we can have dinner together?"

Tommy shook his head. "That's mighty nice and all but like I said, this town don't forgive or forget. Your life here will be better without me. I'd best be heading out."

Darcy stood up. "Where will you go?"

He smiled wryly. "I'm not sure yet, but you don't have to worry about me I'll be just fine. Take care of yourself, Darcy." He turned and began walking away.

Darcy sat and watched him, his figure growing smaller and smaller with each step. She blew out a long breath and then looked down at Rebel. She scratched his head and tried to quell the gnawing feeling growing in the pit of her stomach. "Oh hell," she muttered. "Come on, Rebel, let's get in the car." Rebel looked up at her and with a small wag of his tail, sprinted towards the car. Darcy climbed in and drove until she could see Tommy's figure slowly growing larger and she came to a stop beside him. He looked at her in surprise. "Get in," she grumbled. "You can stay with me." Tommy started to open his mouth then closed it again. He climbed into the car and Darcy made a U-turn, heading back in the direction she came from.

Chapter 12

"You did what?" Colin shouted, standing outside of Frank's Diner, glaring at Darcy.

"I'm letting Tommy stay with me, just until he gets on his feet."

Colin shook his head. "Damn it, Darcy, you didn't hear a word I said, did you? That man is nothing but trouble. He beat your mom and you think it's a good idea to invite him into your home."

Darcy glared at him. "I don't recall asking for your permission or your opinion, Sheriff."

Tommy was calmly sipping his coffee and watching through the front window at Darcy and Colin yelling at one another. *That girl sure is a spitfire*, thought Tommy. *She's the spitting image of her mama and has her daddy's temper.* He couldn't help but be glad his daughter had inherited some of his qualities. He watched the way Darcy's eyes blazed when she was passionate about something. The way she stood tall and staunch.

Tommy stood up and walked outside. He wasn't about to have Darcy fight his battles for him. He cleared his throat and then said, "Sheriff, we were having us a nice breakfast before you interrupted us. I'm sure

Darcy, myself, and all the other patrons would like to get back to it, if you don't mind."

Colin took his eyes off Darcy and gazed at everyone staring at him through the window. His eyes landed on Jack who had a grin on his face, then he looked back at Tommy. He was about to say something, but instead placed his hat on his head and stomped off. Darcy walked apologetically back into the diner and took her seat across from Tommy. Miranda came over and topped off their coffee before moving on to the next table.

Tommy scowled and said in a low voice, "See what I mean about this town never forgetting, and they sure as hell won't forgive. You're better off without me. It's not too late to change your mind."

Darcy locked eyes with Tommy and said, "I'll decide if I'm better off without you." She picked up her fork and dove into her eggs. "For now, let's just enjoy our breakfast, shall we?" She could feel people glancing at them and whispering. She saw Jack paying his bill and walking out of the diner. She quickly wiped her mouth and mumbled, "I'll be right back." She hastily walked out the door. "Jack!" she yelled. Jack stopped and turned around. Darcy ran up to him and said, "I was wondering if I could come by for another shooting lesson sometime soon."

Jack was quiet for a moment. He looked past her in the direction of Tommy, then said, "Darcy, you are welcome to come by any time, I mean that, but I suggest you not bring Tommy along with you. He's not welcome on my property."

Darcy shrugged. "That's fine. I'll be over this afternoon."

Jack nodded then continued on his way.

Darcy went back inside. Tommy looked at her. "Can I ask you something?"

"Sure."

Tommy continued. "Who was that man you were with the other day?"

Darcy laughed. "Please don't tell me you're going to try and be a father now."

Tommy laughed uncomfortably. "You're a big girl. If you're anything like your mama, then you have no problem taking care of yourself."

Darcy looked proud. "Yes, I can. But to answer your question, his name is Adam. We're just friends. That's all."

Tommy nodded. "What does he do for a living?"

Darcy swallowed a cup of her coffee and said, "He's a real estate agent."

Tommy looked at her in surprise. "Are you thinking of selling the cabin?"

Darcy laughed. "Probably not but there's a company that wants to buy it, tear it down, and make the property into a resort."

Tommy laughed. "People have been wanting that land since way back when your mom and I were still in high school."

Darcy grimaced. "Well, Adam made me an offer and I told him no. I don't like the idea of the cabin being torn down and a resort popping up, you know? I haven't been there long but that place already feels like home to me."

Tommy took a bite of his eggs. "I understand. I used to feel the same way. Then I learned that home was wherever your mom and you were, and sometimes home is where you make it. Are you thinking of not going back to Seattle?"

Darcy shrugged. "I don't know. At times I miss Seattle but then I look over at the lake, breathe in the fresh air, and stare at the mountains and I know that if I go back, I'm really going to miss this place and if I sell, I won't have a place to come back to."

Tommy wiped his mouth as Miranda came to take his plate away. "If you don't mind me asking, how much are they offering? It's gotta be in the millions by now."

Darcy shifted uncomfortably she wasn't ready to discuss money with Tommy. "It's a fair offer. Are you ready to go?" she asked, quickly changing the subject. Tommy didn't answer but stood up and followed her out of the diner.

The ride home was quiet, each lost in their own thoughts. As Darcy pulled up in front of the cabin Tommy commented, "You know, this place has a lot of bad memories for me, but it was always home for your mama. It's seems a bit run down but if you don't mind, I can help you make some repairs." Darcy studied the cabin and noticed the roof was starting to sag and she still needed a new front door. Scanning her yard, she noticed that the cabin wasn't the only thing that needed tending to. Weeds grew rampant in front of the house where no doubt there used to be rose bushes and bright colored flowers. "It's the least I can do for you letting me stay here. I'm not a freeloader. I can't pay you with money but I can pay you with my time."

Darcy thought for a minute; she didn't want Tommy to get the wrong idea. This was supposed to be a temporary arrangement. "Since we don't know how long you're staying, I'll take you up on your offer. I suppose there are a few things that can be fixed up."

Tommy laughed. "A few?" She looked so serious watching him. He stopped laughing and said, "I hear you loud and clear. I won't overstay my welcome, but I will help fix up the place. I think maybe we should start with the roof?"

Darcy looked at the sagging roof and sighed. "That might be a good place to start. Let me know what supplies you need and I'll place an order tomorrow." Darcy walked inside as Tommy took the ladder and climbed up on the roof.

Darcy changed her clothes and grabbed the rifle that she kept under her bed. Rebel was at her heels as she stepped outside.

Tommy's heart skipped a beat as he spied Darcy coming out of the cabin carrying a rifle. He shouted down at her, "Are you planning on shooting me with that thing?"

Darcy looked at him seriously and answered, "Only if you give me a reason to." Tommy nodded then Darcy laughed. "I'm just kidding. I'm going out to shoot for a while."

Tommy shouted down to her, "Would you like company? I can't own firearms, but I can keep you company."

Darcy shook her head. "No thanks, I like to shoot alone. It relaxes me."

Tommy shook his head. "If you say so. Have I ever told you that you remind me a lot of your mother?" Darcy just smiled as she opened the door for Rebel and headed out to Jack's.

Chapter 13

Darcy and Jack were sitting across from each other at the old picnic table cleaning their rifles. "Do you have any kids, Jack?"

Jack laughed bitterly. "I have a son, but we don't quite see eye to eye. He doesn't come around and I don't impose. I was a different person back then and believe me, I don't blame him for not sticking around."

Darcy looked at Jack sympathetically. "Sorry to hear that." She started reassembling her rifle when her phone rang. She glanced down in surprise. "Hello?"

The voice on the other end spoke. "Hello, Mrs. Blackwell, this is Mr. Glenn from Camp Wheaton. There's been an altercation and I'd like to speak to you about Emma."

Darcy's heart felt like it was going to jump out of her chest. "Is she all right?" she asked, standing up.

"She's fine, Mrs. Blackwell, but we really need to talk. How soon can you get here?"

Darcy stood up, panicking. "I'm on my way." She hung up and looked wildly at Jack. "I've got to go something has happened to my daughter."

Jack stood up. "I'll drive you." Darcy looked at all the pieces of the rifle still sitting on the table. "No Jack,

I'll be fine. I feel bad asking you this, but can you finish my rifle for me? I really need to go."

Jack shooed her away. "Go, go! Just be careful. I'm sure everything will be okay."

Darcy nodded and quickly grabbed her keys. Rebel was by her side as she ran to the car.

"You have got to be kidding me!" Darcy groaned when she pulled over to the side of the road as the flashing red and blue lights pulled up behind her. Colin got out and walked up to the driver's side window. "Really Colin? Right now, is not a good time!"

Colin shook his head, "Do you know why I pulled you over?"

Darcy slammed her car into park and shouted, "Gee, Sheriff, could it be because you enjoy making my life a living hell?"

Colin took off his sunglasses and tried to use his restraint to remain professional. He almost pulled it off until he saw the defiance in Darcy's eyes. "Damn it, Darcy, I'm just doing my job. You were speeding through town. Can I see your license and registration, please?"

Darcy glared. "I've gotta go. Emma's in trouble."

Colin handed her license back and said, "Why didn't you just say that? What kind of trouble?"

She ignored his questions. "So, you're letting me go?"

Colin shook his head. "No but I will drive you. I can't in good conscience let you continue to drive erratically." Darcy was about to argue but didn't want to waste any more time. She and Rebel got out of the car and Colin cleared his throat. "Why don't you leave Rebel here with your car, and I'll call my deputy to bring them both back to your house."

Darcy hesitated, she didn't want to leave Rebel behind, but she grudgingly admitted to herself that Colin's suggestion made the most sense. She locked her car and hid the key then climbed into his cruiser. "What airport are we going to?" Colin asked.

Darcy looked at him confused. "Airport?"

Colin explained. "Isn't that the fastest way to get back to Washington?"

Darcy shook her head trying to understand. "Why would I go to Washington? I need to go to Malstrom Naval Base."

Colin cleared his throat. "Oh, when you said you were from Washington. I just figured that was where the camp was located."

Darcy shook her head in astonishment. "I can't believe you would think I'd send my daughter to a camp in a different state. What kind of parent do you think I am?"

Colin held up his hand in surrender. "Okay, okay, I'm sorry. In my line of work there's not much that surprises me. So, is this camp located on the base?"

Darcy nodded. "Yes, it's open to kids whose parents are or were in the military. This was Emma's first year going."

"Oh, so this is like a grief counseling camp?" Darcy shook her head. "Not quite. It's a self-defense camp. I figured since her dad isn't around to help protect her, and as much as I want to, I can't hover over her and protect her from the big bad world, she should be able to protect herself as much as possible."

Colin was impressed. Emma was a lucky girl to have such a smart mom. He asked, "What's Emma like?"

Darcy smiled and he could see the pride on her face as she thought of her daughter. "She's very smart and not only in the book smart way. She's inquisitive and is always asking questions, and if she's not satisfied with the answer, she'll investigate further until she is. She's beautiful—"

Colin interjected, "Exactly like her mother." Darcy was stunned into silence until Colin said, "Tell me more about her."

Darcy looked out the window at the trees whirring by in a blur. She could feel the panic beginning to build in her chest again. *What happened? They said she's not hurt but then why am I racing up there?*

"Darcy?" Colin asked. "Are you okay?"

Darcy hastily wiped away the tears that were beginning to fall. "Can't this thing go any faster?" she asked.

Colin looked at her. "Not if there isn't an emergency."

Darcy looked at him incredulous. "This is an emergency! My daughter could be hurt. She's probably wondering what is taking me so long to get to her. Please, Colin, I'm begging you. Drive faster!"

Colin shook his head and whispered under his breath, "Damn it, Darcy!" He turned on the lights and sirens and sped down the road. When they neared the base, he turned off the lights and pulled into the visitors' parking area. Darcy showed her ID and explained why Colin was there.

They were both escorted to a camp located on the west side of the base. Darcy immediately jumped out of the car and headed towards the front door of the office, Colin followed behind feeling uncomfortable and wondering if he should just stay in the car. It really wasn't any of his business, after all, but as he watched Darcy's body stiffen the closer, she got to the door, his instincts told him she was bracing herself for the worst and there was no way he'd let her face that alone. So, he followed, and he would be there for her come hell or high water and knowing Darcy, it was going to be hell.

He sat in one of three metal chairs that lined against the wall as Darcy approached the receptionist. She gave her name and the receptionist placed a phone call before standing up and leading Darcy through a solid wooden door that held a gold name plate with the name, Mr. Glenn, secured squarely in the center. As Colin sat patiently in his seat waiting, a young girl entered the room. He knew immediately that it was Emma because she was a spitting image of Darcy. She looked warily at him and took the chair beside him.

"I can't believe they actually called the cops on me." Colin tried to suppress his laugh. "So how does this work?" Emma asked.

"How does what work?" Colin asked.

Emma held out her wrists. "Aren't you supposed to cuff me and read me my rights?"

Colin folded his hands and leaned on his knees so that he was eye to eye with Emma. "That depends. What are you in for?" he asked, keeping up the charade.

"I beat the crap out of Bobby Duglan."

Colin nodded his head. "So, assault and battery. That's a pretty serious crime."

Emma nodded in agreement. "I know, but you don't know the whole story."

Colin leaned forward. "Why don't you tell me."

Emma looked at him uncertainly and said, "Well, Julie and I were down on the pier fishing and Bobby and some of his friends came down and started making fun of Julie. He was calling her stupid and fat and ugly. Julie started crying, and this wasn't the first time that he's done this. Well, then his friends started laughing at her and calling her names. I told them to leave Julie alone and Bobby started walking towards her. Then he pushed her in the water, and she doesn't even know how to swim. Luckily, the water wasn't really deep, and she could stand up. I was so mad I went after Bobby, punched him in the stomach and broke his nose." Colin looked at her stone faced. "I know what I did was wrong," Emma continued. "but to be honest, I'd probably do again. So, can you arrest me now before my mom comes out here?"

Colin looked confused. "Why?"

Emma looked at him like he was crazy. "Because once my mom comes out that door, she's going to kill me. So, I'd like to be gone before that happens."

Colin knew the phrase "she's going to kill me" was just an expression, but the cop in him had to ask. "Does your mom hurt you?"

Now Emma looked at him as if he were insane. "What? No! It's worse."

"How could it be worse?" Colin asked.

Emma sighed. "It's the look."

Colin squinted at her. "The look?"

Emma rolled her eyes. "Yes, the look. You know. The look moms give you, like the 'Just wait until we get home' look, or the 'You are so grounded' look, or the 'I'm so disappointed in your actions'. You know 'the look'."

Colin laughed then tried to act serious. "Oh, I know the look all right. She's given me the 'You can't be serious' look quite a few times."

Emma laughed. "Oh yeah, she uses that one a lot. That's the one where she lifts one of her eyebrows and opens her eyes wide. It looks like she's shooting daggers at you."

Colin did laugh that time. "Yep, that's the one."

Emma was quiet for a moment as she heard her mom's voice beginning to rise. "Officer, can I ask you a question?"

"Sure."

"When they're done talking, they're going to make me go in there with them. Will you go with me?"

Colin eyed her with concern. "Why would you want me to go in with you?"

Emma looked embarrassed but said, "Well, you're a policeman and they probably won't yell at me too bad if you're there."

The door opened quickly and Darcy stood glaring at her daughter. The man beside her said, "Emma, come in please."

Emma looked at Darcy and mumbled under her breath to Colin, "Oh man, it's all the looks put together. This is bad."

Colin chuckled then stood up.

Darcy looked at him and said, "Colin, could you just wait out here, please."

Colin shook his head. "I'm sorry, Darcy, but Emma here has requested that I accompany her into this meeting. It's my job to protect the innocent."

Darcy's eyebrow shot up and her eyes grew wide as if she were about to shoot daggers. Both Emma and Colin looked at each other and burst out laughing. Emma took his hand and led him into the office.

Darcy didn't have time to argue so she glared at Colin. Darcy looked at Emma. "Emma, Mr. Glenn, told me you were fighting with some of the kids here at camp."

Emma rolled her eyes. "Can you please hear my side of the story?"

Darcy looked at her daughter with concern. "I believe I know the story. Did you hit another person?"

Emma looked angry. "Yes, but there's a good reason." Darcy looked first at Colin and then at Mr. Glenn.

She turned towards her daughter. "Tell me why you would do such a thing?"

Emma looked relieved, but Mr. Glenn interrupted. "I've got another meeting in ten minutes. I'm sure you can explain on your way home. The fact is that you engaged in physical fighting and the consequence of such action is expulsion from the camp."

Emma looked shocked and, Colin noted, very pissed off, which was exactly the same look that her mother had on her face at the moment. "Mr. Glenn," Darcy said, in an even voice. "I sat here and listened to the facts according to your perspective and I think it's only fair that I hear what Emma has to say. As for your 'meeting' in ten minutes, that will have to wait. You called me and scared the life out of me because I thought something was wrong with my daughter, so Colin and I raced up here with lights and sirens blaring."

Mr. Glenn and Emma both looked at Colin. Colin shrugged, Mr. Glenn rolled his eyes, and Emma looked impressed. Colin decided that he liked that look on her.

"So," Darcy continued, "with all due respect, I'd like to hear what my daughter has to say."

Emma looked relieved that Darcy was willing to listen, and although Mr. Glenn already heard her side of the story, she was glad her mom was trying to be fair. Emma repeated the story she told Colin almost word for word.

Darcy looked first from Emma to Mr. Glenn, then to Colin, then back to Emma. "So, you did this because you were defending a friend who was being bullied and harassed?" Emma nodded then Darcy looked at Colin who also nodded. That was all Darcy needed before she erupted on Mr. Glenn. "So, what you are saying is that it's okay to bully and harass someone, but it isn't okay to help the victim?"

Mr. Glenn spoke in a matter-of-fact tone of voice. "Mrs. Blackwell, the fact is that this is a self-defense camp for kids. We will not tolerate any physical altercations. It's simply not acceptable or safe for that matter. Now, you and your daughter both signed contracts agreeing that if a physical altercation took place, then she would be expelled."

Darcy couldn't argue with that and instead asked. "What happened to the other person involved in this incident?"

Mr. Glenn looked Darcy in the eyes and said evenly, "It was dealt with accordingly."

Darcy leaned forward. "Was this person expelled as well?"

Mr. Glenn responded, "That is confidential. We are discussing the consequences of your daughter's action."

Emma spoke up. "No, he wasn't expelled. He's the son of a master chief petty officer."

Darcy let out a sigh. "Well, that explains a lot." She looked at Emma. "I'm proud of you for helping someone in trouble. Let's get out of here." Darcy, Colin, and Emma stood to leave.

Emma looked at Mr. Glenn with the same determined look that her mother had and said, "He's going to do it again, you know." Darcy put her arm around her daughter as they all walked out the door.

Emma looked at the police cruiser parked in the parking lot. She looked questioningly at her mom. Colin quickly intervened. "Emma, you're going to have to sit in the back seat. It's the rules. Technically your mom should be in the back too, but I will leave that up to her." He looked over at her and could see that she was sticking by Emma's side. They both climbed in the back as Colin sat behind the wheel. He backed out and listened to Darcy as she was directing him off the base.

"There he is!" Emma cried out.

"There who is?" Darcy asked.

"Bobby Duglin, the one that kept picking on Julie."

Colin studied the boy as he slowly drove by. Bobby Duglin was sporting two black eyes and a swollen nose while walking with two other lanky boys. All three boys were walking down the sidewalk, pushing each other and fooling around. Colin turned on his lights and quickly pulled over.

"What are you doing?" Darcy hissed.

He looked at Darcy in his mirror. "I'm just doing my job." He put on his hat and looked over his shoulder towards Emma. "Emma, can I count on you to be my backup?"

Emma grinned from ear to ear. "Oh yeah!"

Darcy looked at them both. "No, you're not Emma. You've already gotten into enough trouble. Colin, can we just go?"

Colin looked from Emma to Darcy. "Not until I've taken care of this." He looked at Darcy. "Stay in the car. Emma and I've got this." He stepped out of the car and then opened the back door for Emma. Colin noticed that for once Darcy listened to him. They walked up to the three boys who were watching them quizzically.

Bobby laughed. "Emma, I'm glad to see you're being arrested. You should be for what you did." The other boys laughed along with him.

Colin walked up to Bobby and said in a very formal voice. "Are you Bobby Dugan?"

Bobby laughed again. "Yes sir, and I want to press charges against Emma for breaking my nose."

Colin pulled out a notebook from his front pocket. "Well, Bobby, Emma here says that you were harassing and bullying a young girl by the name of Julie." His eyes slid to Emma who spoke up.

"Cabott. Julie Cabott."

Colin wrote down Julie's last name as to not forget. "Is this true, young man?"

Bobby looked at the officer, wide eyed and innocent. "No, sir. My friends and I were just talking to each other and minding our own business when Emma," he pointed accusingly, "hauled off and attacked me for no reason."

Colin kept a straight face and continued writing. "So let me get this straight, you are saying that this little girl here beat you up?" Emma snickered and Colin gave her a warning look. She stopped and stood quietly by his side.

Bobby mumbled, "It wasn't like that."

Colin squinted. "Then what was it like?"

Bobby looked at his two friends for back-up, but they were no help. "I didn't even see her. She just came out of nowhere."

Colin shook his head and laughed a little then he said, "I see." His smile quickly faded then he leaned over so he was eye to eye with the boy and asked in a serious voice, "Do you have any witnesses?"

Bobby puffed out his chin. "Yes." He pointed to the two boys who were standing by quietly, looking petrified.

"Okay, gentlemen, it's your turn. May I remind you that lying to an officer is an obstruction of justice?" He looked at the two boys and said, "Can I have your names, and I will also need the names of your parents."

Colin could see the petrified look change to full blown panic.

One of the boys cleared his throat and looked at his friend. "I didn't see anything, sir."

The other boy joined in. "Neither did I."

Colin glared at Bobby. "I see. Well then, you best be on your way since this doesn't pertain to the two of you." The two boys turned and fled without looking back. Colin looked back at Bobby. "Son, I think it's time I spoke with your father. Lying to an officer and bullying are serious offenses."

Bobby glared at Emma. "Tell him," he yelled, motioning to Colin. "Tell him the truth."

Emma shrugged. "Okay. Julie and I were on the end of the dock fishing and out of nowhere he," she pointed to Bobby, "started calling Julie names and bullying her. He started running towards her and Julie started crying and screaming. She was begging him to leave her alone then he pushed her off the dock into the water. I may have punched him, but I did it because he was going to hurt Julie. She doesn't even know how to swim. Now he's trying to blame this all on me."

Colin looked back at Bobby and said, "Well, son, I'm going to need to speak with your father." Colin could swear the boy started turning from red faced, to white, to ashen.

"Please, Officer, don't tell my dad. I won't do it again I promise."

Colin believed the boy, but he also knew that he wouldn't let Emma leave this base without understanding that sometimes the good guys win. Colin shook his head. "This is a very serious matter and your father needs to know. I could give you a ride to your house if you'd like."

Bobby looked like he was going to pass out right there. He shook his head no and Colin nodded, kind of feeling sorry for the kid. "Okay then," he said. "We will follow you, but no funny business, or you'll be in more trouble than you're already in."

Colin and Emma walked back to the car and Colin started slowly following Bobby. Emma was laughing hysterically in the backseat. "Shhh," said Colin. "He'll hear you."

Darcy shook her head. "I can't believe the two of you are scaring that boy. Don't you think he's learned his lesson?"

Colin looked in the rearview mirror. "Not quite, but he will."

They pulled up in front of his house and Bobby walked inside to get his father. Colin and Emma got out of the car. Darcy was going to follow until Colin said, "Damn it, Darcy, stay put. You're gonna blow our cover."

Emma looked sympathetically at Darcy. "You really will, Mom. We've got this." Colin and Emma walked towards the house, where Bobby's dad met them at the front door. Bobby was standing beside him now, looking a putrid green.

Colin introduced himself and Emma and then looked at Bobby. "I believe you have something to tell your father." Emma could swear Bobby looked like he was about to pass out.

She almost felt sorry for him. Bobby looked at Colin and then at his father. "I was teasing Julie Cabott," the boy mumbled. Bobby looked from his father to Colin hoping that would be good enough, but he could see that it wasn't. "Justin and Peter were with me. Anyway, I guess you could say we were bullying her, and I pushed her off the dock."

Before the master chief could say anything, Emma interjected. "She didn't know how to swim."

That just made the master chief look even angrier. He looked at his son. "I guess the story about you running and tripping over a stick and breaking your nose was a lie." Bobby couldn't make eye contact and instead looked away and nodded in affirmation. His father spoke again. "So how did you break your nose?"

Emma spoke up. "I did it, sir. I'm sorry, but I just couldn't stand by and do nothing."

"I see," said Master Chief Duglin, glaring at his son. "Well, young lady, a job well done. I'm glad to see there are young people who still believe in right and wrong." He looked at Colin and held out his hand. "Thank you, Officer, for bringing this to my attention, and believe me, I will be taking care of this situation and it will not be happening again."

Colin shook his hand and looked at Bobby. "I'm glad to hear it."

Then the master chief bent over and looked at Emma. "I don't condone violence, but I also know that sometimes there are exceptions. I'm proud of you for what you did for your friend. You are a brave young lady."

Emma smiled. "Thank you." She took Colin's hand as they both walked back to the car. Darcy was astounded. She had never seen her daughter so trusting of anyone since her dad died.

Emma talked non-stop for the first hour of the trip home. Oh, how Darcy had missed this. She looked up to see Colin watching them in his rearview mirror and smiled.

Chapter 14

As Emma rattled on, Darcy's thoughts drifted to the cabin. Now that Emma wasn't in camp any more, some decisions had to be made. She refused to put her daughter in danger, but she also hated to leave. She looked at Colin as he listened to Emma tell stories from camp, and every so often interjecting to ask a question. He had a kind face and when he smiled his dimples would show. His dark hair was cut short and he had a five o'clock shadow beginning to appear. His thick neck led to strong muscular shoulders and...

"Isn't that right, Mom?" Colin looked in his mirror at Darcy and saw her face begin to turn red.

"Right about what, sweetheart?"

Emma rolled her eyes. "Right about spending the rest of the summer at the cabin."

Darcy tried to hide her apprehension and instead said, "I don't know. I'm pretty much done at the cabin. I thought you'd want to get back home to see all of your friends."

Emma's face took on a stubborn look and Colin raised an eyebrow, wondering who would win this battle of wills. Before either one had a chance to say anything, he interrupted. "We don't need to make that decision tonight, do we?" They were both quiet and he knew that in both of their minds they were developing their argument to either stay or go. He could see the conflict in Darcy's eyes and knew she was thinking about how the threats against her were becoming more dangerous. He knew she wouldn't put Emma in harm's way and neither would he, but he also didn't want to see her go. There was something about Darcy that attracted him. Maybe it was those green eyes or sensuous lips that he had been aching to kiss. No, he couldn't let her disappear from his life.

Emma was speaking again. "Colin how did you and my mom meet? Did you arrest her?"

Colin laughed and Darcy huffed indignantly. "No, Emma, I did not arrest your mom. Believe me, there was a time or two when I wanted to, but she didn't break the law, she was just being stubborn."

Emma laughed and Darcy replied, "He's a bit nosy."

Colin responded indignantly, "I just like to know what's going on in town. It's part of my job." Then he quickly changed the subject before Darcy could respond. "Emma, you must have gotten your sweetness from your dad because it sure didn't come from your mom." At the mention of her dad the car grew silent. *Shit!* Colin thought.

The car went silent until Emma spoke up. "Did you know my dad?"

Colin cleared his throat and regretfully replied. "No, I didn't but I bet he was an amazing guy though."

Emma asked, "Why do you think that?"

Darcy was speechless, watching the two interact.

"Well, from what I know about you and your mom, I can tell you are both independent, strong willed, and very smart. Your dad had to have been an amazing man to have both of you in his life. Your mom doesn't seem the type to settle for anything less." Colin hesitated for a minute and then asked, "Am I right?"

Emma shrugged. "Probably. Do you know what else my dad did that was amazing?"

"What?" Colin asked.

"My dad was a third time champion at the Mason County Rodeo. Wasn't he, Mom?"

Darcy nodded and smiled. "He sure was and you have the belt buckles and trophies in your room to prove it."

Colin smiled and saw Emma close her eyes and noticed that Darcy wasn't far behind. He kept driving thinking about how nice it was to feel part of a family. He hadn't felt that way since his mom passed away. He didn't realize how much he missed it until now. He continued driving as the sky changed from blue to pink to purple, and then stars began peeking through a blanket of black. He was tired by the time he pulled onto the gravel road towards his house.

He turned off the car as the two sleeping in the back began to wake up. "Are we here?" Emma asked.

Darcy adjusted her eyes and looked at Colin quizzically. "No, honey. This is Colin's house. Why are we here?"

Colin hoped Darcy would play along until he could explain. "I'm tired and my house is closer than yours. I thought we could just sleep here for the night and then I'll take you home in the morning."

Emma yawned and said, "Please, Mom. Can we stay? I'm so tired."

Darcy knew something was up because Colin had to drive by her cabin to reach his house. Suddenly the reason struck her and she met Colin's eyes. *Tommy was at the cabin.* She groaned. "Why not. Let's go."

Darcy tucked Emma into Colin's bed and then walked out to the kitchen where she could smell coffee brewing. She sat down at the kitchen table and gratefully took the cup from him.

Colin sat down across from her and said, "Darcy, I have an idea and I want you to hear me out before you say anything." Darcy looked suspiciously at him but was too tired to argue. "You can't go back to the cabin with Emma. It's too dangerous, what with someone trying to scare you away and Tommy being there." Darcy looked at him ready to defend Tommy when Colin held up his hand. "Just hear me out. Until Tommy proves to me, or to you for that matter, that he is legit and honestly wants to build a relationship with you, I think it's best if Emma isn't around him."

159

Darcy nodded in agreement. She really wanted to believe in Tommy, but he hadn't earned her trust and she definitely didn't want her daughter around him. She sighed, "So what do you propose?"

Colin took a deep breath and said, "You and Emma stay here."

Darcy shook her head adamantly. "That's not possible. Emma's going to wonder why we aren't at the cabin and to be honest I don't trust Tommy in the cabin alone."

Colin took a sip of coffee then put down his mug. "I agree with you. Just hear me out. What if you and Emma stay here and I'll stay at the cabin with Tommy? If anything else happens I'll be there, plus I can keep an eye on Tommy."

Darcy thought about it and then asked, "What am I supposed to tell Emma when she asks why we're staying here and not at the cabin?"

Colin took a sip of coffee and then replied, "You tell her about the chimney fire and explain to her that no one can stay at the cabin right now. She doesn't have to know it was arson."

Darcy leaned back in her chair. "There's only one problem with this plan of yours."

Colin looked concerned. "What's that?"

Darcy said smugly. "If the cabin is uninhabitable then how can you stay there?" Colin was about to say something when she held up her hand to stop him. "You win. We'll stay here with you," Colin's eyebrow rose and she continued. "For Emma's sake."

Colin smiled grateful that for once they wouldn't argue about this. "Of course, for Emma's sake."

Darcy yawned. Colin rose to rinse out their mugs and said, "I'll take the couch, why don't you go on to bed."

Darcy reached out and touched his hand. "Thank you, Colin, for everything."

Colin stopped working and looked into her eyes. "You're welcome."

The next morning Darcy woke to the sound of Emma and Colin laughing in the kitchen. "I'll scramble the eggs and you cook," Emma instructed.

"That also means you catch," challenged Colin. Darcy, still in her rumpled clothes padded out to see Colin tossing an egg to Emma who easily caught it and they both laughed. Darcy leaned against the wall just watching them. She hadn't seen Emma truly laugh, that belly guttural laugh, in so long. It was nice watching her be a kid without the weight of the world on her shoulders. Colin turned his head to see Darcy standing there. On a whim he yelled, "Catch," and tossed an egg to her. She fumbled the egg, being caught off guard but, in the end, saved it from hitting the floor. "Impressive," Colin commented, giving Emma a wink.

Emma laughed. "Yeah, my mom's got skills."

Darcy laughed and brought the egg over to Emma. "Is there anything I can do to help?" she asked.

Emma looked around with an air of authority. "You could set the table, and since you're the last one up you get clean up duty."

Colin looked at Darcy and with a serious tone in his voice said, "You'd better hurry up. Breakfast is ready."

Darcy shook her head in stunned disbelief as they both looked at her expectantly. She smiled and pulled out the plates as Colin and Emma sat down at the table.

All three of them bantered back and forth through breakfast. Darcy laughed so hard at one point that she had to wipe her eyes. Darcy couldn't remember the last time she had enjoyed a meal so much. It had been such a long time since she let her guard down and enjoyed the moment.

Emma took a bite of her eggs and asked, "When do we get to go to the cabin?"

Darcy looked from Colin to Emma and then felt a pang of guilt as she told her daughter the first lie, she'd ever told her. "About that... I didn't want to worry you, but the day before I came to get you, I started a fire in the fireplace, and it resulted in a chimney fire."

Emma's eyes grew huge. "Are you okay?"

Darcy smiled. "I'm fine, but the cabin has a lot of damage. I'm having it fixed but we can't stay there until everything is safe."

Emma frowned. "Does that mean we're going back to Washington?"

Darcy cleared her throat and slowly said, "That's one option, or Colin has been generous enough to let us stay here until the cabin is ready."

Emma's eyes gleamed and she squealed in excitement. "Oh my gosh! Stay here of course."

Colin grinned happily, "I'm glad. I could really use the company."

Emma looked around. "Do you live here by yourself?"

Colin replied, "I do. This used to be my parents' house and now it's mine."

Emma nodded. "Are your parents still alive?"

Colin's eyes became sad, and he said, "My mom passed away three years ago. My dad is still alive, but we don't get along so it's just me, Dusty and Rosie."

"Who're Dusty and Rosie?" Emma asked.

Colin smiled. "They're my horses."

Emma's eyes widened and she looked first at Colin and then at her mother. "He has horses!" she exclaimed. "Can I ride them?"

Colin looked at Darcy and scratched his head. "Well, that would be up to your mom."

Darcy smiled. She knew how much Emma loved horses. "Of course, you can ride one," Darcy replied, "but we aren't going anywhere soon so can we please finish breakfast first?"

Emma rapidly finished her food and placed her dishes in the sink. She went into the bedroom and pulled some clothes out of her suitcase that she had taken to

163

camp. By the time she came out, Darcy was handing Colin the last dish to dry and wiping off her hands. They walked out to the barn and admired the horses. Emma squealed in delight.

Darcy put the brakes on right then and there. "Emma, these are the ground rules. You can ride only if an adult is with you. These horses are fairly tame, but you never know if something will come along and spook it while you're riding. Do you understand?" Emma looked serious and nodded.

Colin handed Emma an apple. "Would you like to feed Rosie?" Emma eagerly grabbed the apple and fed the horse. She slid her hand along Rosie's nose. "She's so beautiful."

Darcy reached over to pet her as well. "She's my favorite. She's very gentle and rides great."

Emma looked up suspiciously. "How would you know that?"

Darcy recovered quickly. "We're friends. Colin showed me his horses and asked if I'd like to go for a ride."

Colin interrupted. "Maybe if it's okay with your mom, we can go riding while she goes to pick up a few things from the cabin."

Emma looked at Darcy. "Can I?"

Darcy nodded in response. Colin smiled at her over Emma's head. Darcy turned and walked out of the barn towards the house and Colin yelled, "Take the jeep, my keys are hanging by the door. We'll drive over and grab your car later."

Darcy smiled. "Thanks! This will be fun!" she said with a wink and Colin groaned.

"Be gentle with her, please."

Darcy pulled up in front of her cabin. It didn't look any different than when she left yesterday. She walked inside and saw Tommy napping on the couch. She walked over and nudged him awake. "Tommy, I thought you were going to start working on repairs around here."

Tommy woke up and yawed. He squinted his left eye and asked accusingly, "Where have you been? I've been up all night worried sick."

Darcy glanced at him then walked towards her room to pack a few things. "Sorry, honestly I forgot you were here."

Tommy stood in the doorway and watched her pack. "Going somewhere?"

Darcy looked at him. "For a few days, but it's nothing for you to worry about. Look, I know I told you that you can stay here until you get on your feet, but I would feel more comfortable if you stayed somewhere else."

Tommy looked confused. "Did I do something wrong?"

Darcy shook her head. "No, you didn't. It's just that after thinking about it, we are, in reality, strangers and I don't feel comfortable with you staying here. Surely, you can understand that."

Tommy tried to control his temper and said with an even voice, "Not really. I mean most people would say we're family but hey, I'd hate to make you uncomfortable." He started walking towards the door. "I guess I'll be seeing you around. I told you people in this town would turn you against me."

Darcy went back to packing. "It's not like that. I just need some time to adjust."

Tommy nodded. "Darcy, it's not that I needed to stay here. Hell, I've been on my own for a long time. I'm worried about you. Someone is sending you a nasty message. I don't want to see anything bad happen to you." Darcy opened her mouth to interject but Tommy held up his hand. "Now before you go arguing with me, just remember that I was here when that message was written on your wall from the blood of that decapitated bird. I've also noticed that a gun sits in the corner of your bedroom where it would be easy for you to grab should the need arise. Hell, Darcy, I don't want to see you shoot somebody and I don't want to see you get hurt or worse." Darcy sat down on her bed, frustrated. "Look," said Tommy, "if you're not comfortable with me being here with you I can understand that. You appear to be going on a trip since you're packing a suitcase. Why don't you let me stay until you get back? Once you get back then I'm out of here, if that's what you still want."

Darcy looked at him and could tell he was being sincere and truthfully, it wasn't safe to bring Emma here but she also didn't want to leave the cabin empty. Darcy held out her hand. "Deal. You can stay until I get back."

Tommy breathed out a sigh of relief. "Thank you," he said. "There's just one more thing." He motioned to Rebel. "Are you taking that mutt with you? He doesn't seem to like me much."

Darcy looked over at Rebel sleeping on the floor in the corner of the room and smiled. "Yes, I'll take Rebel with me." She zipped up her suitcase and walked towards the door. Rebel stood up and began to follow her. She stopped and turned around. "Thank you, Tommy, for staying here. I really mean it. I do want us to get to know each other but it's gonna take some time and I hope you'll stick around for us to do that." She closed the door behind her.

Chapter 15

Tommy watched Darcy through the window and ran a relieved hand through his hair. *At least she didn't kick me out,* he thought to himself.

"Tommy," a deep voice rang out behind him.

Startled, he jumped. "Jason, what the hell are you trying to do, kill me?"

Jason walked in and made himself at home on the couch. "I saw that cop's jeep here and figured you had company. Turned out I was right."

Tommy eyed him suspiciously. "What do you want ?"

Jason walked to the refrigerator and reached for two cans of beer. He carried them back to the couch, handed one to Tommy, and opened the other one for himself. "Well for starters," ordered Jason. "You need to stay in character. You should be calling me Adam. I'm just here to see how our plan is going?"

Tommy looked at him and mumbled, "I need more time."

Jason looked at Tommy. "Look, Tommy, I know I told you I'd help you out because you had my back in prison, but we're running out of time here. Mr. Weston wanted me to deliver a message if I happened to see you."

Tommy pulled out a cigarette and struggled to light it with his shaky hands. "Oh yeah?" he replied. "What's the message?"

"He wants his money by the end of the week. If you don't deliver on either the money or this piece of property, then it's over."

Tommy began to fidget. "I need more time! C'mon, Jason, you know me. Have I ever let you down?"

Jason walked over to Tommy. "It's not me you have to worry about now, is it? I wasn't the one who gambled my life away, and I mean that literally. We need to get moving on this!"

Tommy walked away so that he didn't have to look Jason in the eye. "Okay, okay, I get what you're saying. I just got her to let me stay here. I need more time to convince her to sign over the deed."

Jason wasn't buying it. "If you can't deliver, then I'm out. I'm not going to end up a dead man. What do you want to do? Do you want me to ask her out again? Do you want me to keep sending her messages? What?"

Tommy ground his cigarette on the counter and said, "Find out where she's hiding. She told me she wasn't going to stay here, and I have a feeling she's shacking up with that cop."

Jason shrugged. "You're the boss. I'll let you know what I find out."

Chapter 16

Darcy smiled as she parked the jeep and watched Colin and Emma brushing down the horses. Colin was laughing at something Emma had said as Darcy walked up.

"Mom, the ride was awesome! I wish you were with us."

Darcy smiled and squeezed her daughter. "Next time, I promise."

Emma looked down next to Darcy's feet. "Where did the dog come from?"

Darcy watched her daughter's face as she announced. "He's ours."

Emma looked at her in surprise. "Oh my gosh! He's really ours? You're not joking are you because this is nothing to joke about."

Darcy laughed and bent down and patted Rebel's side. "Yes, he's ours. Colin thought we needed a dog if we were going to be spending time at the cabin. I mean there are wild animals lurking about."

Emma stared at her mom. "So, Colin got us a dog? When?"

Darcy knelt down closer to Rebel so she wouldn't have to look at Emma. "I've had him for a few weeks now. I wanted to surprise you."

Emma hugged Rebel. "Well, you did! What's his name?"

Colin had been watching Emma's reaction and smiled. "His name is Rebel."

Emma looked at the dog. "Well, Rebel, let's go feed the horses."

Darcy and Colin watched until Emma was out of ear shot. "Well, how did it go?" Colin asked.

Darcy walked towards the house beside him. "Well, I'm packed. I had a talk with Tommy, and I told him that he could stay."

Colin looked at her astounded. "What! Damn it, Darcy, I thought we agreed he needed to go."

Darcy rolled her eyes and huffed clearly irritated. "I know, but when I told him to leave, he actually made a very good point. Someone should be staying there. What if something happens to the cabin and no one is there to protect it? I told him that he could stay for as long as I'm gone, after that he needs to go. He agreed."

Colin was quiet and by the look on his face he was furious. "I could have taken care of the cabin. We've gone over this."

Darcy wasn't backing down. "I still want you to solve this case, but you can't be in both places at the same time. This way Tommy can keep an eye out for anything suspicious, the cabin will be fixed up when we

171

move back into it, and you're free to concentrate on your job."

Colin looked past Darcy towards Emma. "I think you should lay low for a while and keep Emma here. The less people know the better. I'll call the station and tell them that I'll be working from home for a few days"

Darcy looked over at Emma. "I think me laying low and you not making your rounds will raise a red flag, don't you? This is a small town, and when I don't show up at the diner, Miranda and Jack are going to wonder where I am. I can't just drop off the face of the earth. I was at Jack's house when I got the phone call about Emma. He'll worry."

Colin shook his head in disgust. "The only thing Jack worries about is himself. You don't have to worry about that one."

Darcy looked out over the field then back at Colin. "I don't know what happened between you and Jack but you're wrong. Our relationship is very different from yours. If you gave him a chance, I think your opinion of him would change."

Colin mumbled under his breath. "Don't be so sure." He cleared his throat and spoke louder. "Do you have a better idea?"

Darcy shrugged and said, "Actually, I do. The only other person besides you that I trust Emma with is Jack. We can invite him out here to keep an eye on Emma. You can go to work as usual and I can still be seen around town so that Weston Enterprises will see that I'm not giving in to their threats."

Colin was already shaking his head in disagreement. "I like your plan except for the part where Jack comes here. That man is not welcome in my home. Period."

Darcy shrugged nonchalantly and replied, "Okay, have it your way."

Colin let out a sigh in relief. "Thank you."

Darcy called out, "Emma honey, let's go inside and get our things, we're leaving."

Emma walked out of the barn, confused. "Leaving? I thought we couldn't go to the cabin for a few days."

Darcy refused to look at Colin. "I know, honey, but with the two of us we'll have the cabin cleaned in no time."

Colin groaned. "Fine, have it your way. I'll talk to Jack."

"Who's Jack?" Emma asked.

Darcy ignored Colin and said noncommittally. "Jack is a great friend of mine and he also happens to be Colin's handyman. He stays on the property and helps take care of the horses and fixes things that break." Darcy shot Colin a reproachful look. "Unfortunately, Colin lost his temper over something silly and fired Jack."

Emma looked from Colin to her mom trying to piece together what her mom was trying to say. "If Jack did something wrong then Colin probably had a good reason to fire Jack even if he is your friend. Why is it so important that Colin take him back?"

Darcy didn't' expect her daughter to take Colin's side over hers. She glared at Colin and then smiled tightly at her daughter. *Since when did she feel she had to explain herself?* "Well, sometimes Colin is grumpy and takes his frustration out on the wrong person. He and Jack had a falling out, but I'm sure they'll work it out. How about some lunch?"

Emma walked over next to Colin and stared at Darcy in disbelief. "I don't believe you, Mom. Colin is a sheriff and I'm sure if he fired this Jack person it was for a good reason. He shouldn't have to apologize to anyone."

Colin interrupted before things got too far out of control. "Emma, although I appreciate what you're trying to do, I think maybe I might have been too hard on Jack." He saw the look of self-satisfaction on Darcy's face and couldn't resist. "I'm not agreeing with your mom. My issues with Jack are justified but I just can't take 'the look'." He looked conspiratorially at Emma and they both started laughing.

Darcy did not see the humor and could tell she was part of an inside joke. Her irritation with him grew but she kept quiet for Emma's sake. Emma ran off with Rebel and Colin's heart swelled with what he pretty much thought was love for this girl. It meant the world to him that she would side with him, not that he was asking her to pick sides of course. Darcy looked hurt when she looked at Colin. "What's wrong now? I said I'd talk to him. What more do you want?"

Darcy's eyes welled up with tears as she looked at him. "It's not you. It's Emma. All this time it's always been the two of us against the world. I've never seen her defend someone against me. I feel like I'm losing her."

Colin wrapped his arms around her. "You're not losing her, Darcy. She loves you, that's plain to see. She's growing up and finding her own truth in right and wrong. She gets that from you. You raised her to be strong and independent in her decisions and to question things she may not agree with. You did that for her and you should be proud. I, for one, am impressed with her ability to think for herself."

She pulled away from Colin and looked at him. "You're right, she is independent in her thinking. I guess I should be proud that she doesn't just take the easy way out." She looked up in his eyes, "Thank you, Colin. It means the world to me to see the way she is with you. If you don't want to let Jack stay here, I will try to figure something else out. I don't want to make you miserable in your own home."

Colin watched Emma throwing a ball for Rebel and laughing when Rebel took off like a shot. "No, it's okay. I will go talk to Jack today. You were right, even when I hate to admit it. Jack is the best person to protect Emma when I'm away."

Darcy hesitated and asked shyly, "Can you wait a minute? I have something for him." She walked into her

175

room, grabbed a sealed envelope, and handed it to him. "Would you please give this to him?"

Darcy recognized the regret in his face. "You had this all planned out, didn't you?" Colin remarked accusingly.

Darcy hesitated. "No, not exactly. I mean I hoped you'd see it my way." He continued to stare in silence until she broke down and said, "Okay, I had a plan, yes, but I wasn't sure how it was going to pan out. I'm just grateful you agreed to it."

Colin put on his hat, shook his head, and took the envelope. "You know, Jack just might say no."

Darcy thought for a moment and replied, "You might be right, but don't get your hopes up about that."

***

Colin walked into the diner and groaned when he saw Jack sitting at the booth, sipping his coffee and reading the paper. He walked over to him and sat down.

Jack put down his paper and asked sarcastically, "Well, Sheriff, to what do I owe the pleasure?"

Colin looked irritated and growled, "Believe me, Jack, the pleasure is all yours. I'm only doing this for Darcy."

At the sound of her name Jack perked up. "Is everything all right? She seemed worried when she left my place the other day."

Colin rolled his eyes. "Don't start acting all concerned, she's fine. She said the letter will explain everything. I don't know what it says but I know what it's about and it's fine with me if you want to do it." Colin slid the letter over to Jack and abruptly got up and left.

Jack opened the envelope and pulled out the sheet of paper.

Dear Jack,

Thank you again for keeping my gun for me and I also assume you cleaned it. I'm in a bit of a spot and I hope that you will be willing to help. That phone call was about my daughter, Emma. She got into a bit of trouble and was expelled from camp. We're at Colin's house because I don't want Emma involved in whoever is trying to get me to sell the cabin. I really need your help, Jack. You and Colin are the only ones I would trust the life of my daughter with. Would you please consider staying here at Colin's with us until this whole thing blows over? I need to keep up the charade that I am staying at the cabin and that I'm still not selling, but I can't do this without your help. Before you say no, I have talked to Colin and he is fine with letting you stay here. I have no one else to turn to, Jack. I really need your help.

Love,
Darcy

"Well, I'll be damned," Jack muttered, rereading the letter.

Miranda looked up. "Did you say something, Jack?"

He looked over at Miranda and grumbled. "Only that I need my bill." He stood up and met her at the register.

Chapter 17

Darcy and Emma stood in the yard throwing a yellow tennis ball for Rebel to retrieve. Emma looked at her mom. "Are we ever going back to Seattle?"

Darcy looked at her daughter with concern. "Of course, we are. What made you think that we weren't?"

Emma shrugged and threw the ball. "Well, to begin with, we're staying at Colin's house and not the cabin."

Rebel came trotting up to Darcy wagging his tail waiting for her to throw the ball. "And I explained why we can't stay at the cabin. This is only temporary."

"I know," answered Emma. "But what about Rebel? We can't keep him in our apartment because they won't let us have pets. I don't want to drop him off at the pound when we leave that's not fair to him. I know we haven't had him for very long but I already love him." Emma's eyes began filling with tears as Rebel came over to nudge her hand for a pet.

Darcy's heart broke for her daughter. She gently pushed her daughter's hair back from her face. "I know, I love him too, but I'm sure Colin will keep him. I don't think he'll wind up in the pound, or maybe Jack can take care of him."

Emma bent down and ran her hand down Rebel's side. She looked up at her mom. "You mean the handyman?"

Darcy nodded and threw the ball again. "Jack isn't just a handyman. I told you earlier that we've become good friends and he was best friends with your great grandpa."

Emma smiled slowly, "Really? They were really best friends."

Darcy nodded, "Yep. They were even in a war together."

Emma looked sad. "Wow, that's cool. I wish I could have met my grandparents."

Darcy looked pensive. "Me too. Jack tells me stories about them. You know, maybe if you ask, he'll tell you stories too." That seemed to cheer Emma up.

Colin pulled into the driveway and turned off his jeep. "Hi, what are you two doing out here?"

Emma pointed to Rebel. "Just playing with the dog. Colin, can I ask you something?"

He tousled her hair. "Sure, Emma, what is it?"

Emma hesitated and asked, "When mom and I go back to Washington, will you take care of Rebel for us?"

Her question caught him off guard. He looked confused when he faced Darcy. "Are you planning on leaving soon?"

Darcy shook her head. "Not until everything is taken care of here. Emma just wanted to make sure that she was leaving Rebel in good hands."

Colin tried to mask his disappointment. Them leaving was the furthest thing from his mind. He studied Emma. "You don't want to take him with you? He's your dog."

Darcy interjected and shook her head. "Our apartment won't allow us to have pets, and even if I could convince the office manager to let us keep him, which is highly doubtful, he'd be miserable staying on a leash or being locked up in an apartment all day."

Colin nodded. "Yeah, I suppose he would. Emma, I promise that I will take good care of Rebel when you leave." Emma squealed and hugged him. He felt awkward hugging her back. He wasn't the touchy feely type, but surprisingly it sparked something within him. He had never wanted children, or a wife for that matter. His life was fine the way it was, but coming home to Darcy and Emma had him yearning for their company. They added a zest for life and infused energy into his very bland lifestyle. He liked it. A lot.

Emma looked down at Rebel and yelled, "Race ya!" The two of them took off like a shot across the yard.

Darcy looked at Colin with concern. "Is everything all right?"

Colin cleared his throat. "What? Yes, everything is fine. Let's go inside, I'm starved."

Darcy started walking alongside him. "So how did it go with Jack?" she asked.

Colin shrugged. "All right, I guess."

Darcy raised an eyebrow and stopped. "What do you mean, you guess? Is Jack coming?"

Colin blew out an exasperated breath. "I don't know, Darcy. I did what you asked. I went to the diner, found Jack, gave him your envelope, and told him it was fine with me."

Darcy pressed on. "Did he say anything after he read what I wrote?"

Colin ran a frustrated hand through his hair. "I don't know. I didn't stick around."

Darcy was livid. "What? Why not?"

Colin started walking towards the house with Darcy trying hard to keep up. "You know I don't like the man. Now he's going to be living in my house? I'm not going to stick around and be friends. If he comes, then he comes and if he doesn't, I'll be thrilled."

He heard a yelp behind him and turned to find Darcy sitting on the ground, holding her ankle. "What happened?" he asked rushing towards her.

"What does it look like?" she snapped. "I fell. I didn't see Rebel's ball; I stepped on it and twisted my ankle." She tried to stand up and groaned in pain.

Colin placed an arm around her back and the other under her knees to pick her up.

Darcy grimaced. "You can put me down. I don't need to be carried."

Colin shook his head. "Let's take a look at it before we jump to any conclusions." He looked into her eyes and felt his heart flutter. *Oh, this is not good.*

Darcy groaned and wrapped her arms around his neck. She laid her head against his shoulders. *God, he smells good.* "I'm sorry I snapped at you," she murmured. "It just hurts, a lot."

He carried her up on the porch and started to gently lay her on a bench. She forgot to let go of his neck and nervously licked her lips. Colin gently put his hand alongside her face. It felt as if a force held them together, their lips a mere whisper apart as Jack cleared his throat. "Am I interrupting something here?"

They quickly jumped apart as Colin glared at Jack and retorted, "You always did know how to mess up a good thing." He stood up and looked at Darcy. "I'll go get some ice for that ankle."

Darcy fidgeted with her hair and smiled in relief. "Jack! Thank you for coming and no, you weren't interrupting anything. You got here just in time."

Colin came out with a bag of ice and gently placed it on Darcy's ankle.

Jack stood awkwardly and nervously looked around. "Where is that amazing daughter of yours, Darcy?"

Darcy laughed. "She's running around with Rebel. We'll give you some time to get settled in first before being bombarded by Emma."

Darcy looked at Colin and then Jack coughed and forced himself to look at Colin. "Where am I settling into?"

Colin grumbled, "Well the sap house hasn't been used since..." He trailed off there then mumbled, "For quite a few years. I'm sure we can put a cot out there for you."

Darcy looked at Colin in disbelief. "He's not going to sleep in an abandoned old sap house." She looked at Jack and smiled. "With any luck, Colin will get to the bottom of this in a few days and your stay can be brief. Would you mind bunking in Colin's room? Emma and I have moved into the spare room."

Jack and Colin both looked at Darcy like she had lost her ever loving mind. "Absolutely not!" Colin retorted.

Jack spoke up. "I have to say I agree with Colin. If it's no imposition, I'll be happy to stay on the couch." Darcy looked at Colin expectantly.

Colin looked past Jack then glared at Darcy. "No, no imposition at all. Make yourself at home. My home is your home. He grabbed his hat and muttered, "I've got to get back to work."

He started walking off then abruptly turned around and went back inside to grab his keys. He slid on his dark sunglasses and stomped down the porch towards his jeep. He paused before he opened the door and said, "Darcy, I'm going to be working late tonight. Don't bother waiting up." He slammed his door and drove away. *That woman had a way of getting on his last nerve.* He shook his head in frustration. Never in his life did he ever envision Jack visiting, let alone staying, in his home. He was going to get to the end of this investigation and Darcy and Jack, both, could get the hell out of his house and he could go back to living a normal, peaceful life.

Emma ran up to Darcy and Jack on the porch. "Where is Colin going in such a hurry?"

Darcy reached for Emma's hand and said, "He had to go back to work. Emma, this is Jack, the man I was telling you about." Emma looked at Jack and smiled.

Jack smiled back and said, "It's nice to finally meet you, Emma. Your mom has been telling me a lot about you."

Emma groaned. "She always does that. So, you're the handyman here, huh? Well, anytime you need help with the horses I would love to help."

Jack laughed. "Believe me I will need help and I'm going to hold you to your offer." Emma grinned with delight and ran inside the house with Rebel.

Jack eyed Darcy. "Handyman, huh?"

Darcy laughed. "Well, your own personal bodyguard seemed a little over the top."

Jack laughed. "Yeah, I suppose you're right. I can pull off the handyman bit, there's no need to worry."

Darcy started to stand up. "I'll help you with your stuff. Ouch!"

Jack jumped up. "No, you just sit. I'm not an invalid. I can get my own stuff. Plus, I'm only moving it to the couch."

Darcy readjusted the ice and sat back in on the bench. She could hear Jack and Emma talking through the screened door. "My mom told me that you were good friends with my great grandfather."

Jack replied, "I sure was. He was a brave and good friend. He even saved my life a time or two, but that's a story for another time." He looked around. "Well, now that I have all my stuff out of my car, what do you say we go out and check on those horses?"

Emma smiled from ear to ear. "I thought you'd never ask." They both laughed together and began to walk towards the barn while Emma was still talking. "Did you know I was at a self-defense camp?"

Jack stopped and looked at her. "You'll have to show me some moves. You know, I was in special ops for a spell in the military. Maybe I can teach you some moves."

Emma looked at him in awe. "I'd love that!" They continued walking towards the horses. Emma grabbed a brush and handed it to Jack. "So, what do you do around here?"

Jack looked at her in surprise. "Well," he said, trying to think quickly, "I keep the stables clean, fix anything that is broken, handyman stuff." Emma nodded.

About an hour later, Jack and Emma were on the front lawn. Emma was showing Jack how to get out of a wrist hold and Jack was showing Emma how to do a round house kick. He was quite limber for his age.

Darcy loved watching them together and was saddened that her own daughter would never have the opportunity to share these moments with her own grandfather. Darcy stood up and started to put a more pressure on her ankle. It still hurt, but nothing a bandage wrap wouldn't help. She limped towards the kitchen to make dinner. This wasn't her house and she wasn't sure what kind of food she would find. After scrounging through the cabinets, she found pasta, spaghetti sauce, and Italian bread. She started boiling water for the noodles and then started the sauce. Emma came walking in and volunteered to set the table.

Jack sat at the table, turning his head and studying the pictures that hung on the walls and sat on stands. There were pictures of Colin with his mom before she got sick. There were pictures of his grandparents and pictures of vacations with friends. He didn't see one single picture of his father, but then again, he didn't expect to.

As the girls sat down to eat, Emma asked, "So, Jack, what did you and Colin have an argument out about?"

Jack huffed and grumbled, "What makes you think we had an argument?"

Emma looked at her mom and then back to Jack. "That's what mom said. She said you and Colin had a falling out and Colin fired you. She sent him out to bring you back."

Jack looked irritated. "Well, the falling out, as you call it, has to do with Colin being stubborn just like his old man." Emma waited for him to continue but he didn't.

They ate lunch in silence until Darcy said, "I have to run to town for a few things, plus I need to stop by the cabin. Emma, would you mind sticking around here with Jack and Rebel? It'll just be a quick trip."

Emma looked at her mom and asked, "Can't I come with you?"

Darcy shook her head. "Not this time, honey." She looked over at Jack for help.

"Emma," Jack said, "remember when you said you'd give me a hand with the horses? Well, part of my job is exercising them. Maybe we can take them out for a ride? It'll go faster with both of us exercising them."

Emma grinned from ear to ear. "Okay." She looked apologetically at Darcy. "Never mind, Mom. You can go. I'll be fine with Jack."

Darcy grabbed her laptop and drove towards the diner. She wanted to investigate Weston Enterprises to see if there had been any complaints about them. Walking into the diner and seeing all the familiar faces felt like home to Darcy. She shook her head and smiled at how much things had changed in the past few weeks. She sat in her usual booth and booted up her computer. While she was waiting, Miranda sauntered up to her and placed her usual cup of coffee down on the table. "Thanks, Miranda," Darcy said with a smile.

Miranda smiled back but looked concerned. "Have you by any chance seen Jack? He comes in for his morning coffee every day, but he hasn't been in today. I'm a little worried about him."

Shit. Darcy thought quickly. "Actually, he's been helping me at the cabin. I had to come in to get some work done," she said nodding towards the computer. "But I promised him I'd bring him his coffee when I leave."

"Whew, that's a relief," Miranda replied. "Has something else happened at the cabin? I can give you a hand after my shift."

Darcy shook her head. "Thanks for the offer but you don't have to. I just wanted to update the plumbing and Jack said he could do it for a lot less than hiring a plumber."

Darcy motioned for Miranda to have a seat which she gladly took. Darcy looked at her friend intently and saw the worry lines around her eyes and the slight frown that she was trying to hide. "Is something else bothering you?"

Miranda slowly looked at Darcy and said nervously, "Darcy, I'm not one to spread rumors or listen to gossip for that matter, and I know this is none of my business, but you're my friend and I care about you."

Darcy looked at her, bewildered. "What's going on?"

Miranda blew out a breath and said nervously, "There's been a lot of talk about Tommy being back in town. Now I know he's your father and all and no matter what, family is family that's what my mama always said. I just worry about you. Your mother kept you away from him for a reason and I don't want to see you get hurt."

Darcy smiled. "You have nothing to worry about. Yes, Tommy has been coming around and yes, he is trying to get back into my good graces, but he has to earn that. It's not going to come easy, believe me. If I feel that something's wrong, I'll be the first one to boot him out of town, trust me."

The door opened and two customers walked in. Miranda squeezed Darcy's hand then left to greet them as Darcy began typing Weston Enterprises into her search engine. She scrolled down and clicked on one of the links. It appeared Weston Enterprises owned resorts in many different states, including Missouri. She continued searching but each link just reiterated what she had already learned. It was a legitimate business and there were no reports of anyone being run off their land, or worse.

Darcy thought for a moment and then typed in 'Tommy Blackwell'. She felt a little guilty not giving her father the benefit of the doubt, but Miranda's words kept coming back to her. As she began searching, she discovered that her father had previously been living in Las Vegas. She continued searching and clicked on a link for public records. She was especially interested in his prior incidents involving the law. It didn't surprise her that he had a long rap sheet prior to being incarcerated for the domestic abuse case involving her mother, but she was surprised that once Tommy had been released there were no other incidents or arrests. In fact, it seemed as though he had lived a fairly quiet and normal life. Maybe he was telling her the truth, she thought to herself. She ordered Jack's coffee and left the diner.

Chapter 18

Darcy drove out to the cabin to check on Tommy. Although she'd found nothing on the internet, that didn't mean she trusted him. She walked into the cabin and found that he wasn't there. She walked outside and didn't find him there either. She looked up and saw that the roof looked significantly better than it did before. She had to admit, so far, he was on the up and up.

She walked out back and looked at the majestic mountains that surrounded her. A blue heron landed near the lake out back. She couldn't imagine giving all of this up. In fact, if she were honest with herself, she couldn't imagine being anywhere else. The temperature was rising and Darcy could feel a bead of sweat rolling down her back. She started walking towards the lake. No one was here, she had the whole place to herself and it was getting hotter by the minute. She stripped down, thinking to herself that the next time she was in town she really ought to buy a bathing suit. The lake was far enough back that if Tommy showed up, he wouldn't see her. She slowly stepped into the lake to allow her body time to acclimate to the cooler temperatures. Once she felt ready, she started to swim. The water was cool and refreshing. She started swimming to the other side enjoying the feel of the water gliding over top of her.

"I thought I might find you here," Colin shouted loud enough for Darcy to hear him.

She stopped swimming and groaned; this could not be happening again. She swam towards him but made sure she was a safe distance away so that he couldn't see that she was once again in her birthday suit. "Oh, hey, Colin," she said hoping to sound nonchalant. "What are you doing here?"

Colin looked at the blue sky overhead, trying to exercise patience. "I could ask you the same thing. I thought we agreed that you were going to let me investigate."

Darcy shrugged which hinted to Colin that she was nude. "I'm not investigating I'm swimming in the lake on my own property. Just came to cool off, that's all."

Colin was starting to sweat, but not from the heat. "Damn it, Darcy, it's not safe for you to come out here all alone. If I didn't decide at the last minute to come out and check on things, I wouldn't even have known that you were here. What if Tommy tried to hurt you?"

Darcy retorted, "Unless you have proof that Tommy is the one behind all this, then I'm going to keep coming out here."

Colin's eyes darkened. "Is that so?"

Darcy lifted her chin in defiance. "That is so, Sheriff."

Colin placed his hands on his hips. "Then I'm placing you under arrest."

Darcy just smiled. "For what, swimming in my own pond? I don't think so."

Colin shook his head. "No, for interfering with an ongoing investigation."

Darcy laughed now. "You can't be serious."

Colin stood taunt and stone faced. "I am serious and you need to come out and get dressed."

Darcy shook her head. "Nope. If you're going to arrest me, then come and get me."

Colin squinted. "You do realize that would also be a violation and you'd be charged with fleeing from a police officer." Darcy stood up and the water was level with her breasts. Colin swallowed hard; he had never felt this way about anyone before. He was treading on dangerous territory. He unbelted his holster and began taking it off. He took off his hat and set it on top of the holster. Then he began to unbutton his shirt.

"What are you doing?" Darcy asked, feeling a moment of panic and attraction at the same time." He slid his shirt to the ground and then lifted his T-shirt over his head. *Oh My God.* His body taunted and beckoned her fingers to trace over his rock hard six pack. She was already envisioning those muscular arms wrapped around her. Next, he unzipped his pants and watched her as he slowly removed them as well. She watched as he finished undressing and saw that he was already starting to get aroused. He looked down and laughed in embarrassment, then he looked at her again with such a burning desire it took her breath away. She hadn't been with a man since John, her husband, but right now, all she knew was how much she wanted Colin. He came into the water and began to swim over to Darcy. She watched him as he came closer and she could feel her breath catch.

Colin cleared his throat and said, "You have the right to remain silent."

Darcy felt as if she had no control in what her body did. She advanced towards him and wrapped her arms around his neck. He pulled her towards him, his eyes never wavering from hers. Colin opened his mouth to continue, but Darcy quieted him by placing her mouth over his.

They kissed tentatively at first, then more passionately. They explored each other's bodies, feeling the heat rise with each touch, each kiss. Colin wrapped his arms around Darcy and pulled her closer to him. She wrapped her legs around his waist and pressed herself against him. She felt him enter her and she gasped. It had been so long since she'd been with anyone. She could feel a dam break within her. The dam that held everyone at bay so she would no longer hurt any more. They moved in unison, kissing, exploring, exploding. They kissed again, tenderly this time.

Colin spoke. "Damn it, Darcy, the things you do to me. I can't get you out of my head."

Darcy kissed him again. "You make me just as crazy. Am I still under arrest?" she asked coyly.

Colin pulled her back in close to him and kissed her thoroughly and she could feel him becoming aroused again. She smiled and was about to begin exploring him a second time as they both heard, "Ahem." They froze and turned their heads towards the shore.

Tommy stood with his hands in his pockets and looked uncomfortable. "I wasn't expecting company," Tommy shouted out to them. They both rapidly pulled away and looked at him.

Darcy shouted back to him, "What the hell are you doing here?"

Tommy replied, "I was going to ask you two that same question."

Darcy and Colin swam closer towards Tommy, but far enough that he didn't get the full view.

Tommy looked at Colin. "I sure bet the taxpayers in this county would be happy to know that our good sheriff here is skinny dipping when he should be protecting its citizens."

Colin glared at Tommy. "I'm off duty and it's none of your business what I do on my own time."

Darcy groaned. "Tommy would you please go back to the cabin and we can talk there."

Tommy squinted towards the sky then shook his head. He sighed heavily. "Sure, come on up when you're ready. I'll make us some coffee."

Colin tried to control his temper at Tommy's sarcastic tone. "No need, Tommy," Colin replied. "I'm heading home."

Darcy nodded. "I'll be up, Tommy, and a cup of coffee sounds great. I want to talk to you about some more repairs that need fixing."

Tommy turned and started walking towards the cabin. He yelled over his shoulder, "You know Darcy, you could do better at picking men."

Darcy yelled back. "You gave up your right to an opinion on my decisions a long time ago, Tommy."

Chapter 19

Darcy sat across the table with a mug of coffee in her hand. Tommy spoke first. "So, what else needs fixing?"

Darcy ignored his question and asked. "Have there been any more incidents on the property?"

Tommy sighed. "Nope. Not a one."

Darcy raised her eyebrows in surprise. "Don't you think it's strange, that since you've moved in here there hasn't been one single incident?"

Tommy glared at her and said evenly, "What are trying to say Darcy?"

Darcy shrugged. "I guess I'm asking if you're the one who's trying to run me off of my land?"

Tommy put down his coffee. "You've been listening to those town folks, haven't you? You really think that I could be the one behind this? Your own father?"

Darcy put down her mug. "Please, don't play the father card. I don't know what to think and no, it's not because of people in town, it's because I'm perceptive."

Tommy got up and placed his mug in the sink. "No, Darcy, I'm not trying to run you off your land. I'm trying to build a relationship with you. I thought we'd been over this." Darcy got up and stood next to him.

"Like I said before, Tommy, I'm willing to get to know you more and possibly down the road build a relationship, but I've gotta warn you. Don't underestimate me."

Tommy chuckled. "Believe me, sweetheart, I've only underestimated one woman in my life and that was your mama. I don't intend to make the same mistake twice."

Darcy smiled tightly. "Good. Now back to what needs fixing. The roof looks good and solid, but I'd like to have a solid front door, preferably one that doesn't have axe marks in the center of it."

Tommy began washing out the mugs. "Will do, boss. I'll get right on it."

Darcy turned to leave. "I'll stop by in a few days. I wouldn't want to surprise you again."

Tommy turned and leaned against the counter. "Good to know. One quick question before you leave?"

"What's that?" Darcy replied.

"What's going on between you and that sheriff? You two sure looked mighty cozy."

Darcy laughed and shrugged, then turned and sauntered out the door.

Tommy brushed a hand through his hair in frustration. He picked up the phone and called Jason. It rang three times before he heard, "Yeah, what's up?"

Tommy replied, "There's been a new development and not a good one. I need you over here now."

Jason groaned. "We need to wrap this up, Tommy. Weston is beginning to lose patience."

Tommy yelled into the phone, "You don't think I know that! Just get over here."

Half an hour later, Jason strolled up to the cabin. "Okay, I'm here. What's going on?"

Tommy handed him a beer and popped one open for himself. "Darcy and our pain in the ass sheriff are becoming quite friendly with one another. I want you to scope out his place and see if she's staying there. If she is, then slash her tires. Let them know that we haven't given up and we know where she is. Leave the paperwork in her car to remind her to sign.

Jason took a long pull of his beer and was quiet for a moment. "I don't like the idea of going to the sheriff's place and I sure as hell ain't going to risk going back to jail."

Tommy threw his half full can of beer across the yard, hitting a tree and sending suds flying everywhere. "Well, I sure as hell can't go out there. They'll lock me up for sure and I'm not going down alone. How about you stay in your car with binoculars and stake the place out. That way, chances are you won't be seen and if you are, just charm Darcy into going on another date with you. C'mon, Jason, help me out here. In a few days this will all be over with. You'll have paid your debt to me and you'll never have to see me again."

Jason liked the sound of that. "Okay, but it has to wait until dusk. I don't want to be out there in broad daylight."

Tommy breathed a sigh of relief. "Thanks, I'll be glad when we can both get far away from this little po'dunk town."

Later, Jason drove his rental car down the road towards the edge of the tree line. He didn't want to be recognized so he pulled his baseball cap down lower. He got out of the car and stood between two tall oak trees. He took out his binoculars and looked through them towards the house. He saw through the window into the kitchen and could see Darcy making dinner at the stove. He scanned the binoculars over the driveway and noted that Darcy's car was the only vehicle in the driveway.

He took a step out of the woods and was beginning to walk towards her car when he saw movement in the house. He slouched down and raced the rest of the way towards the car before he could be spotted.

"Emma, time for dinner!" Darcy shouted from the open doorway, then she turned to go inside.

The sound of Emma's voice came from inside the barn. "Coming, Mom!"

Jason hunched behind the car trying to catch his breath and nearly jumped out of his skin when he heard, "Who are you?"

He looked up to see the young girl staring down at him. He cleared his throat and tried to sound normal as he said, "I'm the sheriff's mechanic and he wanted me to make sure everything was okay with your mom's car."

Emma squatted down next to him, peering underneath. "Is it?" she asked.

He looked at her blankly. "Is it what?"

Emma looked at him again. "Is her car, okay?" He pretended to look at the tires and said, "Yes, everything seems to be in order. You'd better hurry on in for dinner before your mom comes looking for you."

Emma stood up and dusted off her hands. "Okay, see you around." She left and went inside. Jason let out a sigh of relief as he heard the little girl running towards the house.

He took out his knife and made a slit into the tread of each tire, then he dropped the paperwork for her to sign on the seat of her car. He turned, staying hunched down and raced towards the woods, thankful that the dark sky would keep him from being seen. Relieved, he climbed back into his rental and drove away. He drove straight back to the cabin. He was going to give Tommy an earful about not telling him about the little girl. It would have been nice to have had that information.

He pulled up in front of Darcy's cabin and Tommy walked out onto the porch. He lit a cigarette and pulled off a drag before asking, "How did it go?"

Jason glared at him. "It's done, but it would have been nice if you'd told me that she had the kid with her."

Tommy looked at him astounded. "What?"

Jason sat down and placed his elbows on his knees. "You didn't know?"

Tommy stood and paced across the porch. "Hell no, I didn't know! Are you sure it's her kid?"

Jason nodded. "I think the word 'mom' pretty much confirmed it."

Tommy shook his head. "Shit, well this complicates things."

Jason smiled at him. "I disagree. I think this just made things a whole lot easier. We use the girl as leverage to get Darcy to sign the papers."

Tommy slowly smiled. "Tell Mr. Weston he is about to acquire a prime piece of property." He threw out his cigarette butt and smiled.

***

The next morning Tommy drove out to Colin's house. He was relieved to see that Colin's jeep wasn't parked in the driveway, but Darcy's car was parked out front with four flat tires. He got out and walked up to the house. He knocked on the door but there was no answer. He peeked through the windows. He knocked again and waited. He jumped when he heard a voice behind him say, "She's out in the barn."

Tommy turned around and saw a tall, graceful looking girl with two dark braids trailing down her back. He blinked again. She was the spitting image of a

203

younger Darcy. He cleared his throat. "Hi, I was looking for your mom. Is she here?"

Emma eyed him skeptically and said again, "She's out in the barn. Do you want me to go get her?"

Tommy shook his head. "No, that's okay. I'll just wait here on the porch until she gets done." He sat down in a rocking chair and looked at Emma. "So, you must be Darcy's daughter."

Emma sat on a chair facing him and crossed her ankles. "Yep, that's me."

Tommy smiled. "Well, Emma, it's nice to meet you. My name's Tommy."

Emma scrutinized Tommy then asked, "How do you know my mom?"

Tommy opened his mouth to speak just as Darcy appeared next to Emma. Darcy glared at Tommy. Keeping her voice even, she said, "Emma, honey, why don't you go inside and start cleaning up for breakfast. I'll be just a minute."

Emma smiled and stopped in front of Tommy. "It was nice meeting you, Tommy."

Tommy smiled. "Likewise, Emma. Maybe we'll meet again."

Emma smiled and walked inside. Darcy walked over to the door and closed it so that Emma wouldn't hear their conversation. She turned on Tommy and hissed, "What are you doing here?"

Tommy gazed up at her and replied, "I could ask you the same thing."

Darcy put her hands on her hips. "What do you want?" she demanded.

Tommy stood up. "Well, for starters, it'd be nice if Emma knew she had a grandfather."

Darcy grimaced. "You're kidding, right? She's not going to know that little tidbit of information for a long time, if at all. By the way, you wouldn't happen to know who slashed all four of my tires, would you?"

Tommy tried to look surprised and stood up. "Your tires were slashed? Darcy, maybe you should sign the paperwork. Your safety and Emma's are more important than a piece of land." He eyed her skeptically. "Why would I know anything about your car?"

She huffed, "You show up unannounced and you're talking to my daughter. Why exactly did you stop by?"

Tommy glared at her and said cynically, "I came to ask if you could pick up some more shingles for the roof? I'm running low."

Darcy groaned. "I can't today, obviously, but I will try tomorrow after I get someone out here to fix my tires. Do you have enough to last until I can get out there?"

Tommy stood to leave. "Yeah, there's plenty I can do today, boss. Sorry I intruded. See you in the morning."

***

Jason was waiting impatiently for Tommy to arrive back at the cabin. Hanging out here made him uncomfortable. Two more days, he thought to himself, then his debt to Tommy would be paid and he'd never have to see the man again.

Tommy pulled up in front of the cabin and got out. Jason stepped off the porch and ran a nervous hand through his hair. "So?" he asked.

Tommy threw his hands up in the air. "So, we move ahead as planned. Tomorrow morning Darcy will be picking up shingles. You nab the girl and I'll take care of the rest."

Jason grimaced. "I'm not going to hurt the kid."

Tommy growled, "Nobody's going to get hurt. It's only until Darcy signs over the property. Hell, at one point she didn't even know about the property, so I don't know why she's so set on keeping it now. You need to drive over to Billings and pick up the supplies we need." He pulled out a wad of bills and handed them to Jason. "Wear a hat and sunglasses when you're shopping, so it will be hard to identify you if they decide to look at the cameras."

Jason nodded and stuck the bills into his pocket. He looked at Tommy. "When this is over with, we're even. You understand?"

Tommy held out his hand to Jason. "Tomorrow this will all be over with and we're even."

Jason shook his hand and left. Tomorrow couldn't come soon enough, as far as he was concerned.

Tommy stomped into the cabin and threw his keys across the room, hitting the wall. That bitch would get what was coming to her. Just like her mama did. He was sick of her arrogance, her feeling entitled to this place. He would burn this place to the ground with pleasure after this was all over with. He walked into the bedroom and spied Darcy's rifle leaning in the corner. Stupid girl wasn't even smart enough to take any protection with her. Taking this land from her would be like taking candy from a baby. He walked over and picked up the rifle. It felt good, solid. He checked to see if the clip was still in the gun and saw that it was. Knowing Darcy, she also had a bullet in the chamber. He pulled back the chamber and saw the gleaming gold bullet ready to be launched through the barrel. He desperately wanted to shoot it, but knew better than to call attention to himself. *Patience*, Tommy thought to himself, *everything will come together in its own due time.*

Chapter 20

Tommy and Jason each sat in their cars hidden on a side road, waiting for Darcy to drive by. Jason's cell phone rang. He looked down and saw that it was Tommy. He answered on the second ring. "Darcy just drove by in her car and she's alone. It's time to move in and get started." Jason opened his car door and got out. He slipped on a backpack full of supplies and quietly started walking through the trees towards the barn. He planned on hiding out there until he could nab Emma. The sheer thought of kidnapping her made him sick to his stomach, but if it helped him get rid of Tommy, then he'd do it. One thing's for sure, he wasn't planning on hurting the kid.

He stopped at the side of the barn and put down his backpack. He breathed out a sigh of relief. "What are you doing?" asked Emma.

Jason jumped and turned around. "What are you doing out here?" he asked.

"I asked you first," Emma said, crossing her arms in front of her chest.

Jason opened his mouth to reply. "Emma, breakfast!" Jack shouted. Jason groaned. *Who the hell was that?* This already wasn't going as planned.

Emma was about to shout back when Jason grabbed her and put his hand over her mouth. She tried to scream, until Jason whispered in her ear, "If you make a sound, I will kill the old man."

Emma went silent. Rebel turned the corner and began to run towards them. The dog was growling and showing his teeth as he set his sights on Jason.

Jason panicked. "Call him off! Now!" Emma froze and didn't move. Tears were streaming down her face. "Damn it, girl, do it!"

Rebel lunged at him and sank his teeth into Jason's arm, not letting go. A shot rang out and Rebel yelped, before falling to the ground. There was blood everywhere. Emma started to scream as Jason tightened a hand around her mouth.

Tommy looked at Jason and ordered, "Get her out of here. I'll clean up your mess."

"My mess? Tommy, this was your plan!" Jason walked briskly towards Tommy, dragging Emma behind him. "You never told me about the damn dog and who the hell is the old man?" Jason wasn't finished but abruptly stopped when he saw the rifle Tommy was holding pointed straight towards his own chest. He glared at Tommy as he turned and swung Emma in front of him, pushing her towards the forest. She stumbled over a tree root and almost fell, but he yanked hard on her arm, forcing her to stumble forward. They reached the road and stopped as Jason tried to catch his breath. He pulled Emma towards his car. She screamed for help as his hand came down across her face. "Shut up! Get in the car!" Emma could feel blood trickling from the edge of her lip. She was trying to hold back her tears and was gulping for air. She started to open the back door to get inside. Jason shook his head.

"In the front," he ordered. "I want you where I can see you." Emma closed the back door and walked around the car towards the passenger's side. She thought about making a run for it but knew it was no use. He had longer legs and his stride was three times longer than hers. She opened the door and climbed inside, making sure that her seatbelt was securely fastened.

Jason pulled out onto the main road and started speeding faster and faster towards their destination. Emma closed her eyes, praying that she wouldn't die. Where was a cop when you needed one? She thought about her mom and Colin. She hoped they would find her in time. She started to panic and tried to slow down her breathing. She focused on what her self-defense classes had taught her. She tried to replay every move, every position, every way possible she could defend herself when she had the chance. She began to feel calmer, knowing she had options.

The car came to a stop and she opened her eyes. In front of her was a cabin with a front porch and two rocking chairs. It didn't look abandoned, so that was a relief. Jason swore under his breath and started the car again. Emma tried not to look terrified, wondering what he was going to do to her. He slowly drove the car past the cabin and parked it in the back, out of sight of anyone passing by. He pulled the keys out of the ignition and looked at Emma. "Get out," he growled.

She obeyed his command and felt her legs shaking beneath her. She stood awkwardly, trying to survey her surroundings. Nothing looked familiar. Jason grabbed her by her arm again and led her up the steps. Her head was still throbbing from when he had hit her. She stepped shakily into the cabin, not knowing what was going to happen next. "Go sit on the couch," he ordered as he went over to the sink and splashed cold water on his face. He could feel bile rising up and the last thing he needed to do was start puking in front of the kid. He could feel his hate for Tommy raging through him and he desperately hoped that in a few hours this would all be over and he would be free.

Emma looked around the tiny cabin. It had a homey feel to it and somehow it felt familiar, but she didn't know why. She scanned the books on the bookshelf looking for some type of clue. She could see little picture frames and strained to see who the people were in the pictures, but they were farther away and all in black and white. Between her pounding head and her panic, she couldn't make out who the people were.

Jason looked over at Emma and saw the bruise starting to form on the side of her face. He also noted the dried blood from her lip. *Damn it, I'm an asshole,* he thought to himself. He took a deep breath and tried to remain in control. "Why don't you go in the bathroom and get yourself cleaned up," Jason instructed. Emma stood up and walked to the door that he had motioned towards. "Just keep the door unlocked," he ordered. Emma walked in and closed the door behind her. She looked in the mirror and was horrified at the reflection staring back at her. She looked around and found a washcloth. She wet it and gently started wiping the dried blood off her lip and chin. Once she had cleaned up, she quietly opened the medicine cabinet looking for anything that might help her defend herself. She was shocked to see her mother's makeup and a couple of her prescriptions for headaches. She was tempted to try something for her head, but decided against it. She needed to keep her mind clear. She walked back into the living room and sat back down on the couch.

Jason was leaning against the counter looking at his phone. 'No Service' kept appearing on his screen. He tossed it on the counter in exasperation. He studied Emma quietly and could tell the girl was nervous. *Good, she'll be less trouble that way*. "Do you want a bottle of water?" he asked. Emma nodded yes, but didn't say a word. He grabbed a bottle out of the refrigerator and walked over towards her. He handed it to her and watched as she shakily unscrewed the top.

"Where am I?" she asked in a soft voice, although she had a pretty good idea of where she was.

Jason looked around the cabin and said, "The cabin. The place that started this whole nightmare and by nightfall, with any luck, it will also be the place that ends it." Jason sat on the couch next to Emma and laid his head back, looking at the ceiling. Emma scooted away from him as far as she possibly could. Jason looked at her in surprise. "You don't have to be scared of me, sweetheart," he said sarcastically. "I'm but a mere pawn in this whole charade. Your grandpa, on the other hand, he's the one I'd be worried about. He is one desperate son of a gun and when you're desperate, you're unpredictable."

Emma looked over at him and said, "I think you may have the wrong person. My grandpa is dead. I've never even met him."

Jason looked sadly at Emma. "I wish he were dead, for both of our sakes, but he's alive and dangerous."

Emma thought about what she had just heard. She and her mom had always been honest with one another. "Why would she lie about this?" Emma shook her head. "I'm sure he's dead. You have the wrong person."

Jason started to speak then realized he was talking too much. "Whatever," he said. "All I know is once your momma signs over the deed to Tommy, everything will go back to the way it was and I can get the hell out of this shit town."

"Wait," Emma interrupted. "Tommy's my grandfather? Mom told me he was the handyman working on her cabin."

Jason grimaced. "Well, she got the working on the cabin part right. Believe me, kid, you're better off without him."

Emma was quiet for a moment then said softly, "He shot Rebel." Tears started trickling down her face and she hastily wiped them away, not wanting to show weakness. "Is he dead?"

Jason looked down at his mangled arm and said, "I don't know, but after what he did to me I sure as hell hope so."

Emma remained quiet trying to gather her composure then asked. "Are you going to hurt my mom?" She tried to sound brave but knew she only sounded desperate and heartbroken.

"Tommy's in charge of your mom, not me. We only want your mom to sign a few papers, that's all. No one will get hurt if your mom does what she's told. I guess the answer to that question is up to her."

Emma nodded, and prayed he was telling the truth.

Chapter 21

Jack jumped at the sound of gunshot and rushed out the
door. "Emma!" he screamed as he raced across the yard.
He reached the front of the barn, leaning against the
wall, and gasping for breath. He was praying that Emma
was okay and that she'd be standing on the other side of
the barn. Adrenaline was coursing through his veins and
then panic. *Shit, I don't have anything for protection.*
He frantically looked around where he was standing and
grabbed a pitchfork. He quietly inched his way around
to the side of the barn. He took a deep breath and looked
around the edge of the barn, praying he wouldn't see
Emma lying on the ground. His eyes surveyed the
ground then his knees buckled when he spotted a small
mound lying at the far end of the barn. Fueled by
adrenaline, he frantically began to run. His heart
stopped when he spotted a pool of blood spreading
rapidly from a still lump laying helplessly on the
ground. His eyes filled with tears. "God in Heaven,
please don't let that be Emma," he whispered. He was
shaking as he ran towards the lifeless lump. He saw a
patch of fur, and felt both relief and anguish to discover
it was Rebel.

He blinked hard, trying to refocus and stay alert as his military training began to kick in. He looked around for a sign, a clue, anything that would lead him to Emma. He noticed two sets of footprints leading to the grass and away from the barn. "Emma!" he yelled again, feeling panic well up inside him. "Emma, scream, yell, do something, anything, so I know where you are and that you're okay!" He strained to listen but heard nothing. He followed the footsteps through the grass, relieved to see there were no blood spots. He hurriedly continued to track each step until they ended at the edge of a road. "Damn!" he yelled in frustration. The asphalt road left no clue about which direction Emma's captors would have taken her. He quickly ran back to the barn and prayed he wasn't too late. He threw the pitchfork to the ground in frustration and frantically pulled out his cell phone.

His hands were shaking as he started to punch in the number. He had just punched in the first digit when he heard a familiar, sinister voice coming from behind him. "I suggest you call Darcy and tell her about her kid. Tell her to go to the cabin right away. That's where she'll find her."

Jack slowly turned around and saw Tommy leaning against the corner of the barn, with his feet crossed at the ankles and his arms crossed casually in front of his chest. Jack tried to refrain from running towards him and beating that smug look off his face, but if he knew one thing it was not to provoke the enemy. Jack stood

216

tall with fire in his eyes and shouted, "Tommy, you ain't never been nothin' but a coward, always hurtin' people who couldn't defend themselves. Let Emma go, leave Darcy be, for once in your life be a man."

Tommy picked up the rifle that had been leaning behind him. "Call her *now!*" He raised the rifle and pointed it at Jack's head.

Jack tried to appear to remain calm and shouted back to Tommy, "You're not going to get away with this!"

He dialed Colin with shaky hands and spoke into the phone. "Darcy, they've got Emma. She's up at the cabin. Rebel's... uh—" He cleared his throat. "Rebel's been shot."

Tommy yelled. "Put it on speaker phone, old man I've got something to say."

Jack pretended to press another button but dropped the phone in the process, which landed next to his feet. He looked at Tommy, trying to keep him talking until help arrived. "Sorry I'm shaky in my old age and you pointing that gun at me doesn't help none either."

Tommy blew out a frustrated breath and said, "You're a stupid man. You should have just done as you were told. You didn't call Darcy, did you? Damn it!" He pulled the trigger and watched as Jack fell to the ground.

He raced back to his car, sweating profusely. This was not the plan. Nobody was supposed to get hurt. Oh well, maybe for once people would take him seriously. Darcy would sign those papers once she found out that her beloved Colin was next. He was going to be free of Weston Enterprises and he'd be damned if he was going back to prison. He threw the gun in the back of his car and jumped into the driver's seat. He was shaking, but managed to start the car. Once he was on the road, he slammed his hand on the steering wheel. "Damn," he yelled. He couldn't wait to get out of this backwoods country. Things had just gotten a lot more complicated, thanks to that stupid old man. He'd never killed anyone before, he was just a small-time gambler, but he felt a sense of pride for killing that old man. He had been a pain in his ass for as long as Tommy could remember just like Darcy's grandfather had been. *Good riddance.*

"Jack!" Colin's voice came from the phone. "Jack!" but there was no answer.

Chapter 22

Darcy was driving home singing along with the blaring radio, with a stack of shingles packed tight in the back of her car. She quickly pulled over when she heard a siren blare and saw the red and white lights of an ambulance race past her in the opposite direction. She had a sinking feeling in the pit of her stomach that something was very wrong. She dialed the number to Colin's house, wanting to make sure everything was okay and that everyone was safe. There was no answer. She could feel panic rise in her chest as she dialed Jack's cell phone. No answer. She was about to make a detour, just to check on things, she told herself, when her phone rang. She sighed with relief, thinking it was Jack. "Hello?"

She heard Tommy's voice on the other end. "Darcy, I'm out of shingles. When do you think you could pick up more?" Darcy turned on her blinker to make a left turn away from Colin's. "I'm on my way to the cabin now. I should be there in about ten minutes."

Tommy smiled. "Good, I'll be waiting for you."

He hung up the phone and glared at Emma. "You're smarter than that old man was. You listen." He looked over at Jason and said, "Hide in the bedroom and don't come out. If there's any trouble back me up."

Jason nodded and did as Tommy had ordered. Emma sat nervously at the table, growing more panicked knowing her mom was walking into a trap. She glared at Tommy and said, "So, I hear we're related, huh?"

Tommy took a swig of beer and replied. "Who told you that?"

Emma shrugged. "Is it true?"

Tommy shook his head and laughed. "Just like your mama, you answer a question with a question. Yeah, it's true. I was married to your grandma. I guess she told you I was dead too, huh?"

Emma nodded.

After a few minutes, she asked quietly, "Why are you doing this? Why do you want to hurt my mom? What did she ever do to you?"

Tommy laughed. "Well, for starters she's a self-righteous bitch, just like her mama." Emma's eyes grew wide to hear the hatred in his voice. Tommy took a deep breath and continued. "Look, all I want is for her to sign some papers and then I'll be on my way. Simple as that. She's been stubborn about it but now, now that you're here, I think she'll be more amicable."

Emma took a deep breath, trying to calm her nerves. She heard a vehicle stop in front of the cabin and hoped it was Colin. Darcy beeped the horn.

Tommy glared back at Emma. "Stay here and keep your mouth shut and this will all be over soon."

She nodded and didn't move. She looked towards the bedroom where Jason was hiding, but didn't see any sign of him.

Tommy opened the door and yelled towards Darcy. "Come in for a minute, Darcy. There's something we need to discuss." Darcy shook her head and put on her work gloves. "No time, Tommy. I've got to get back."

Tommy shook his head and laughed, then he turned back towards Emma. "Get out here," he ordered. Emma stood up and did as she was told. The shocked look from Darcy was all the confirmation Tommy needed, to know that he had the upper hand. "Like I said, sweetheart, come in. We've got things to discuss." Emma tried to run towards her mom, but Tommy caught her arm and pulled her back. "I don't think so. You stand right here next to your grandpa."

Darcy cringed at the word but kept her face staunch. She looked at her daughter and asked, "Are you okay Emma?"

Emma nodded as tears trickled down her cheek. "I'm okay," she said, trying to sound brave.

Darcy glared at Tommy and said, "Well, Tommy, what is it that you want to talk about?"

Tommy smiled and said, "Let's go inside." Darcy followed them inside, and Tommy pointed at the table. "There's some paperwork over there that I need you to sign."

"Then what?" replied Darcy. "Are you just going to go on your merry way?" Tommy looked at her calmly and said in an even tone, "That's the plan. Pretty simple, isn't it? Look, I don't want anyone to get hurt. You're my family and I'm yours, whether you want to accept it or not. I just need to even up a debt and then you'll never have to see me again."

Darcy didn't believe him for a minute and was trying to stall, although for what she didn't know. Colin didn't even know she was there, and she was sure he had no idea that Emma was being held hostage. She looked at her daughter then around the cabin. The rifle lay on the counter next to the sink. If only she could get to it.

Tommy followed her eyes to the rifle and he said in a sinister voice, "I wouldn't get any ideas if I were you. Let's just get this over with." He stood up and pulled Emma up with him. He put his arm around her neck, making her a human shield knowing Darcy wasn't that stupid.

"Mom?" Emma begged, as she began to cry harder. Darcy took a shaky breath and walked over to the table. It was the deed to the house and property. She shook her head in disbelief.

She looked at Tommy. "This? This was worth losing your daughter and granddaughter over? A piece of land? Hell, Tommy, from what I've been told there weren't many good memories for you here."

Tommy tightened his hold on Emma. "Just sign the papers, Darcy. Don't play the family card, it's not going to work."

Darcy shrugged. "You're right Tommy. There is no family card. Okay, where do I sign?" She leaned over to pick up a pen. She began to feel relieved when she heard sirens growing louder and getting closer. She knew they were coming to the cabin. Darcy looked out the open door and saw a police car abruptly stop in the yard. She sighed with relief. "It's over, Tommy. Give it up."

Tommy shook his head. "It's not that easy, sweetheart. I thought you were smarter than that. Get out there and tell him to leave." He grabbed the rifle and pointed it at Darcy. Emma screamed uncontrollably and Colin was out of his car instantaneously.

Darcy slowly walked out onto the porch with her hands up. "You need to go, Sheriff. He's got Emma and he's holding a gun."

Colin wasn't listening. He motioned for her to run towards him. She refused to move until she heard the blast of a rifle behind her. Her whole world stopped in that very instant as she thought of her daughter. She turned, running at Tommy who was standing in the doorway, screaming with rage from somewhere deep inside, then stopping abruptly when she found herself looking down the barrel of her own rifle.

Tommy cursed, then said, "Sign the papers, Darcy." Darcy looked at Emma who was still in one piece. She glanced around confused then saw Colin lying on the ground bleeding. She sank to the ground, unable to move. "Get *up!*" Tommy shouted again.

Darcy stood shakily, wiping her tears away, and walked back into the cabin. She angrily picked up the pen and scrawled across the signature line. "There," she said defiantly. "You got what you wanted. I hope it was worth it. I swear, Tommy, I will hunt you down and kill you."

Tommy grinned. "No need to be like that, Darcy. It's just a simple transaction." He looked at her and then said, "Get in your car and leave. When I'm far enough away, I'll tell you where you can pick up your daughter."

Darcy blurted, "I guess the townsfolk were right."

Tommy stopped and glared at her. "Right about what?"

Darcy smiled sympathetically. "You're a no-good coward that can't be trusted."

Tommy's face went hard, and he yelled, "Go, before I change my mind, Darcy." Darcy turned and walked towards her car. Emma wanted to shout after her not to leave, but she couldn't find her voice. Her mom was really leaving.

Darcy started her car, but she wasn't planning on going anywhere without her daughter. She just needed to bide her time until Tommy put down the rifle. She slowly backed out of the dirt driveway and began to drive away. She knew she didn't have much time, because once Tommy saw that she had scrawled 'Fuck

You' on the signature line, it would be all over. She pulled over to the side of the road once she was sure she was out of sight. She climbed out and began searching her car for anything she could use as a weapon. She felt something hard underneath her seat. She pulled it out and smiled. In her hand she had found a 9mm pistol that Colin must have slid under her seat after her tires were fixed.

She got out of her car and walked back towards the house. She pressed her back against the side of the cabin and waited for Tommy to come out. She heard him scream her name once he saw what she had written on the deed. He stormed out the door, dragging Emma beside him.

Darcy stepped out from where she was standing and pointed the gun at Tommy. He glared at her, then pulled Emma in front of him. "Go ahead, Darcy shoot. Watch as your little girl goes down."

Darcy didn't say a word. She just stood frozen watching him, waiting for the right time. Tommy glared at her. "You always were a stubborn one. Why couldn't you just sign the papers, you stupid girl. It didn't have to come to this."

Tommy turned his head and yelled for Jason. Jason didn't appear. He swore under his breath.

Emma tried to motion to her mom that she could make a break for it. Darcy watched her, trying not to let anything show on her face. She tried to distract Tommy.

"Okay, Tommy, I'm done listening to you babble. Just hand over my daughter and you won't get hurt."

Tommy started to laugh, loosening his hold. "It's not me you have to worry about."

Emma seized her opportunity and struck the point of her elbow hard into his groin. Tommy bowed over and let go of Emma. She turned and kicked his knee and she swore she could hear it crack. She ran over to Darcy and stood next to her.

Darcy's eyes didn't leave Tommy. "Emma, check on Colin."

Emma ran over to Colin and knelt next to him. "Is he okay?" Darcy asked.

Emma looked at Colin's pale face and put her hand on his chest to feel if he was breathing. He was wearing a Kevlar vest but was bleeding from the shoulder. "He's bleeding from the shoulder," Emma shouted back.

Darcy clicked off the safety. "Which one? The left or the right?"

Emma looked again and said, "The right shoulder."

Darcy nodded and said, "Turn your head, Emma, and plug your ears."

"Why, Momma?" Emma asked.

"Just do what I say, Emma. Everything is going to be okay."

Tommy's eyes found Darcy's and he said smugly, "You're not going to shoot me. You don't have the guts."

A shot rang out and Tommy screamed in pain, laying on the ground bleeding from his right shoulder."

Emma shouted, "Mom, stop! He's not worth it!"

Darcy looked at Tommy in disgust as he laughed at her. She stepped closer until she was standing right over him. She pointed the gun again, towards his other shoulder, ready to fire.

Tommy grinned up at her. "I dare you."

Emma got up and ran to her mom trying to pull her away. "Mom, Colin's trying to say something!"

She paused, but her eyes never left Tommy's, she heard Colin's voice, weak but insistent. "Damn it Darcy, don't play his game. He'll suffer more in jail than you killing him."

Darcy looked at Tommy with hatred. She pulled back the gun. "You'd better be right, Sheriff."

She walked towards her daughter who ran into her arms, and they both knelt beside Colin. He motioned to his phone and she dialed 911. "Please send an ambulance right away, officer down."

He smiled at her as he heard Tommy yelling, "What about me? I need an ambulance. You saw her, Sheriff. She shot an unarmed man. You're going to be right beside me in jail, Darcy. Do you hear me?"

Colin grimaced as he shouted back to Tommy laying on the porch, "I saw Darcy shoot you in self-defense and you shot me. Do you honestly think for one minute I would vouch for you?"

Tommy groaned. "I wasn't holding a gun. Darcy shot an unarmed man. You're sworn to uphold the law and tell the truth."

Colin closed his eyes as the sound of sirens got louder and louder.

Chapter 23

Darcy and Emma stepped into the hospital room, each carrying a handful of colorful balloons that said, 'Get Well Soon'. Darcy laughed upon seeing Jack and Colin sharing a room. Both men were scowling and each slowly inching up the volume on their separate televisions to hear over the other one. Darcy walked over to Jack and kissed him on the cheek, then she did the same to Colin. "What a coincidence, that you were both shot in the shoulder. I'm glad it wasn't worse."

Jack looked at Darcy and grumbled, "He was a terrible shot. That boy couldn't hit the broadside of a barn if he tried."

Colin interjected. "Well, your injuries may not have been too serious, but he did hit you. I can't believe you didn't take anything to protect yourself with."

"Listen here, Mr. High and Mighty, I may have not done it your way, but looking at your condition, you didn't fare so well yourself." Colin opened his mouth to argue the fact, but Jack waved him off and looked back at Darcy. "I'm sorry I let you down, Darcy. I know you were counting on me to keep Emma safe."

Darcy held his hand and saw his pain reflected back at her. She said gently, "Jack, you did everything you could. I don't blame you. In fact, if you didn't run out there when you heard Emma shouting, who knows how this would have turned out?"

Emma looked from her mother to Jack, confused. She sat on Jack's bed with her arms crossed at her chest. "So, you weren't just the handyman?"

Jack let out a gruff laugh. "No, sweetheart I'm no handyman."

Emma smiled despite herself. "That's a relief. I mean no offense, but you really didn't fix much, in fact sometimes you made things worse." Everyone burst out laughing. Emma's face grew serious. "I did appreciate you teaching me those self-defense moves. It was probably what saved me."

Jack's eyes grew serious again. "Are you sure you're all right?"

Emma nodded and gave him a smile.

Darcy walked over and put her arms around Emma. "See, Jack, you did protect her and me too, for that matter. Thanks for the shooting lessons, they came in handy. Does your shoulder hurt much?"

Jack smiled and shook his head. "It takes a lot more than a little flesh wound to keep this old vet down. I'll be just fine."

Colin cleared his throat and spoke up. "Darcy, we've got to talk about you shooting Tommy."

Jack intervened. "If you charge her, Colin, so help me—"

Colin groaned then growled in anger, "Dad, let me say what I gotta say!"

The room went silent and everyone was staring at Colin. Emma was the first to speak. "Dad? Jack's your dad?" Everyone remained silent looking at Colin. Stunned,

Darcy turned and looked from Colin to Jack and saw that Jack had a tear trickling down his face. She glared at Colin and walked over to Jack and looked down at him with concern in her voice. "Jack, are you all right? Are you in pain?"

Jack wiped his eyes. "No, nothing like that. I just never thought I'd ever hear him call me Dad."

Colin pushed the button on his bed to help him sit up a little more. He looked over at Jack and cleared his throat. "Yes, I called you dad. Now don't go getting all soft on me. I'm not saying everything is sunshine and roses, but you did save the woman I love." He looked up at Darcy and then at Emma. "And hopefully one day my future daughter."

Everyone was speechless, until a quick knock on the door broke the spell and the doctor walked in, smiling at both men. "Good news, gentlemen, you are both getting discharged. Sheriff, I recommend desk duty for two weeks and Jack, just try to stay out of trouble."

Darcy smiled. "That's great news. I'll bring around the car while you two get dressed."

Both men stood up and started to get dressed. Jack cleared his throat and uttered, "So I guess I don't need to stay at your place any more, since you caught Tommy."

Colin chuckled and said, "The doctor said to stay out of trouble, so you're coming back to the house where we can keep an eye on you."

Jack shook his head and smiled. *Maybe there was a chance for them after all.*

Darcy pulled up in front of the hospital as both men sat in wheelchairs, each with a nurse standing behind them. Now that they were side by side, Darcy could see the family resemblance.

Jack climbed in the back next to Emma and Colin was about to climb into the passenger seat when his phone rang. "Hello," he said, as he stood outside the car. His voice was all business. "Are you sure?" he listened for a few minutes and replied, "Thank you for the information. I'll check it out." Then he hung up.

They were quiet on the drive home, each person lost in their own thoughts. Once they got home, Jack went inside to lay down. Darcy put on a fresh pot of coffee and Emma headed for the refrigerator. Colin sat down at the table and asked, "Darcy, when you were at the cabin was there anyone else there besides Tommy?"

Darcy looked puzzled and replied, "No, only Tommy, Emma, and me. Why?"

Colin blew out a long breath and said, "Tommy claims that he didn't kidnap Emma. He says a man by the name of Jason Rutledge did."

Darcy shook her head. "No, that can't be right. I'm sure Tommy was the only one."

Emma sat down at the table with a slice of cold pizza. She shook her head and responded, "You're wrong, Mom. Jason was there and he was the one who took me. Tommy told him to hide in your room when you pulled up."

Darcy and Colin looked at her in disbelief.

"What?" asked Emma.

Darcy looked confused. "Why didn't you say something?"

Emma responded, "Well, there hasn't been much time. Plus, once they arrested Tommy I kind of forgot about Jason. Tommy was definitely the one who was calling the shots."

Colin spoke up first. "When the police searched the cabin, they didn't find any sign of anyone else."

Emma shrugged. "Maybe he climbed out of a window or something. Jason was definitely the one who took me." She touched her bruised face. "And hit me."

Darcy looked at Colin and saw his face darken with rage. He walked over and hugged Emma, then put on his hat and walked towards the door. "Where are you going?" Darcy asked. "You're supposed to be taking it easy, remember?"

His face looked as if it were chiseled in stone and his reply was ominous. "It's not me you have to worry about."

Jack threw off his blanket and hastily grabbed his clothes. He started shuffling towards the bathroom as Darcy walked towards him, with her hands on her hips and asked, "Now what do you think you're doing?"

Jack looked at her dumbfounded and grumbled, "What does it look like I'm doing? Colin's gonna need back up."

Darcy walked towards him, arms crossed, and replied in an even voice, "The only place you are going is back to bed and you're going to take it easy. Doctor's orders."

Jack stopped walking and looked at Darcy. "Woman, I haven't been married in thirty something years and my son may need my help. Now you can move out of my way or I'll move you out of the way, but either way I'm going."

Darcy looked at Jack and frowned. She couldn't lose the two men who held a place in her heart. She stood quiet for a minute then said, "Well, I guess I can't argue with you, but you should probably get dressed first."

Jack smiled in victory then grimaced in pain. Darcy looked worriedly at Emma, knowing Jack didn't have the strength to be of much help to Colin. Jack walked the rest of the way to the bathroom and closed the door. After what seemed like forever, he opened the door and tried to mask his immense pain that shot through his shoulder with every move. He tried to smile victoriously as he walked back into his bedroom and closed the door behind him.

Emma whispered to Darcy, "You can't let him go like that."

Darcy sighed. "I know." She looked at her daughter and whispered, "Here's what we'll do. I'm going to leave right now. I think Colin is headed to the cabin. You stay here with Jack, because he's gonna be angry when he finds out I'm gone. Can you do that for me?"

Emma nodded and then jumped as the doorknob to the bedroom twisted. "Go!" Emma whispered, and suppressed a giggle.

Darcy raced out the door and continued running until she reached her car. She was out of breath as she started the engine and squealed out of the driveway. Luckily, it didn't take her long to catch up to Colin. He spotted her in his rearview mirror and muttered under his breath as he pulled over. He opened his door and walked towards her car.

"Damn it, Darcy what do you think you're doing?"

She smiled sweetly up at him. "I thought you might need help, since you can't use your arm," she said, motioning to his shoulder.

He looked up towards the sky and then back at her. "I'm a police officer, Darcy. I can take care of myself. I have been trained, which I'd like to remind you is not the same kind of training as your training."

Darcy continued smiling and said, "I've been taking care of myself long before you came into my life.

Haven't you ever heard the phrase 'Don't mess with a mama's cub'? This involves me too, Colin, and if you think I am going to sit on the sidelines and wring my hands then you've got another think coming, buster."

Colin groaned. "I don't have time to argue. Follow me, and for the love of Pete, slow down!" Darcy gave him a salute and rolled her window back up.

She followed him the rest of the way to the cabin and parked alongside his patrol car. He motioned for her to stay in the car and pulled out his gun. He banged on the door. "Police!" he yelled as he stood to the side of the door with both hands on his weapon. There was no answer. He looked at Darcy and motioned for her to continue to stay in her car then he started walking towards the back of the cabin. He spotted a window open and used the barrel of his gun to move the curtain aside, so as to not disturb the crime scene. The room was empty. He walked back towards the front of the cabin and saw Darcy letting herself in the front door with her keys. "You were supposed to stay in the car!" he yelled.

"I didn't hear any gun shots, so I wanted to open the door before you busted it down."

Colin shook his head in exasperation. "You watch too much television, but since you're here, we might as well take a look around." Darcy opened the door and they both walked in. Everything still seemed to be in place except that there were more dishes piled in the sink.

Darcy walked into the bedroom and her heart sank. "Someone destroyed my room. Why would anyone do that?" They both stood and stared at all her dresser drawers pulled out and tipped over, and the contents lay strewn all over the floor, bedding thrown to the ground, and clothes lying everywhere. Darcy started to walk into the room.

"Don't go in there," Colin ordered. He pulled out his phone and called the station. "I need someone to drive up here to Darcy's cabin. We've had a break in. It could possibly be Tommy's accomplice."

Darcy sat down at the table before her knees gave out. Her hands were shaking so she held them in her lap. Colin sat down across from her. "Is there anything in particular the perp could have been looking for?"

Darcy shook her head. "Not anything I can think of. In the top drawer was a yellow envelope I had found, full of old letters that my mother had sent back to my grandmother unopened. In it there were also old family photos, newspaper clippings, and a map of the property. There was nothing of significance that anyone would want to steal."

Colin started writing down everything that Darcy was saying. "Can you think of anything else that was in the room? Think hard, Darcy."

Deputy Holtz arrived and walked towards the kitchen where Darcy and Colin were sitting. "Hi, Sheriff, you needed a swipe of the crime scene?"

Colin cleared his throat. "That's right. We have a strong suspicion that whoever broke into Darcy's cabin is directly connected to the crimes that Tommy committed."

Deputy Holtz walked towards the bedroom and began taking pictures of the open window, clothes lying on the bed, and miscellaneous contents strewn all over the floor. He also spotted muddy shoe prints that were tracked along the floor.

Once he was finished, he walked back into the kitchen and sat down. Darcy handed him a mug of coffee. "Thanks," Deputy Holtz said appreciatively. "After this cup of coffee, I'll start dusting for fingerprints. We'll do the whole room, but where do you want us to start?"

Colin looked at Darcy and she replied, "The window was pushed open, my dresser drawer was dumped out and it looks like he rifled through the contents that are lying on my bed." The deputy made a note of it and then finished his coffee. He placed his mug in the sink and picked up a bag with all of his tools in it.

It felt like forever before Deputy Holtz came out of the room. He looked at Colin. "Well, I've got a few good prints, not only footprints but also fingerprints. Hopefully one will lead us to our guy. When I get back to the office, I'll start running them."

Colin stood up and shook the deputy's hand. "Let me know if you find anything."

"I will," Deputy Holtz said, as he tipped his hat towards Darcy and left.

Colin looked at Darcy and said, "You're free to move around the room now, but it's extremely important to notice if anything is out of place or missing. Darcy sat down on the bed and picked up the large yellow manila envelope. She lifted the flap and poured out the contents. Several old pictures fell out. Many of them were black and white. She held up a photo of a tall thin woman with dark bouffant hair. She was smiling, with her hand on the shoulder of a young girl around nine years of age. The little girl had long dark hair with straight bangs. There was no mistaking that it had to be her grandmother and Darcy's mom, since she looked exactly how Darcy had looked as a child. A tall, lanky man in denim overalls standing next to the woman had to be her grandfather. He wasn't smiling, but he had a kind face.

She sorted through the pictures, not recognizing a short dark-haired man next to her grandfather. "Who's that?" she asked.

Colin looked closer at the picture. "I don't know but Jack might know, why don't we take that one back to the house?" Darcy set the picture aside and picked up the stack of letters.

"What are those?" Colin asked.

Darcy smiled sadly. "It's unreturned letters from my grandmother to my mom. Apparently, my mom had no desire to reconnect with her parents. It's too bad they never made amends."

Colin shook his head sadly. "Just like Jack and me. If only we weren't so stubborn, we wouldn't have wasted all these years."

Darcy agreed as she opened one of the letters. She started reading it to herself. then began reading it out loud:

Dear Kim,

I know you have been returning my letters, but I hope and pray you open this one. Your father is not well. He has stage four cancer and will not be with us much longer. He wants to talk to you before he passes. Please, Kim, give him one last chance. Give him peace in this life before moving on to the next. We both miss you so much and want to see you again. I know what Tommy has done to you and I know that he is in jail. I know that you are a single mother trying to raise a child on your own. You don't have to. Come home and be with your family. I would love to meet my granddaughter and become a part of her life. There are so many things I need to tell you. Please sweetheart, if there is a God in Heaven, please come back home.

Love,

Mom

Colin and Darcy sat in silence for a minute, trying to process what they had just read. Colin looked at

Darcy. "I'm sorry you never got a chance to meet your grandmother. You would have loved her."

Darcy's eyes began to fill up with tears and she felt one trickle down her cheek as she hastily wiped it away.

Colin cleared his throat. "I wonder what she needed to tell her?"

Darcy looked up confused. "What do you mean?"

Colin pointed at a sentence in the letter and read, "There are so many things I have to tell you."

Darcy shrugged. "Who knows, and unfortunately we will never know now."

Colin looked down at the stack of letters and said, "Maybe it's in one of these letters. We need to find out what it is. It might give us a clue as to why Tommy was so set on getting this land. Surely, he could have conned someone else for the money he owed Weston Enterprises."

Darcy sifted through the stack of envelopes and stopped when she came to another black and white photo. "Look at this," she said, handing the photo to Colin. He smiled when he saw Darcy's grandfather and Jack, their arms around each other's shoulders, standing proudly in their military uniforms. They were both smiling for the camera, right before they were shipped out to Vietnam. Colin never saw that side of Jack. The Jack he knew as a kid was always angry or drunk, or both. Darcy opened another envelope and pulled out the letter.

Kim,

If you are reading this then that means I am no longer living. You are a stubborn one, I'll give you that. I suppose you get that from me. I know we've had our problems over Tommy and we've both made mistakes. I'm sorry that you felt that you couldn't confide in me and I'm sorry that you felt as though you had to choose between him or me. Now that I'm gone, your momma is going to need some help around here. I'm not just talking physical help but she's hurting in a way that only a daughter could soothe.

There is also something else, there are some people who want our land and they are going to bully your momma until they get it. Please don't let that happen. She's a strong woman, I'll give you that, but these companies will resort to whatever they think they need to do to get what they want. I didn't put it in the will because the less people who know about it the better. These mountains that surround us are filled with gold. I don't care about money or being rich. I never did. I care about this beautiful land that God blessed us with where you can watch wild horses come down to the lake for a drink at night. Where you might call home one day. I love you, Buttercup, and I always will.

Love,
Dad

Darcy wiped a tear from her eye and looked up at Colin. "I can't believe my mother never read these letters. She would have found peace, forgiveness, and would have probably had a relationship with her parents. *I* would have had a relationship with my grandparents." She dropped the letter on the bed and looked at Colin. "I need a break. I can't do this right now."

Colin picked up the letter and read it again. He carried the letter into the kitchen and placed it on the table. He watched Darcy as she wrapped herself in a blanket and sobbed quietly. He knew what it was like to lose family, but Jack was still alive, and that relationship could be mended. He walked over to the counter and started brewing a pot of coffee. He waited for it to stop and brought her over a mug.

She smiled gratefully. "Thank you."

He took a sip of his own and watched her body start to relax. "Better?" he asked.

"Much," replied Darcy.

He paused for a minute. "Did you know that you were sitting on a gold mine?"

Darcy shook her head. "I had no idea."

They were both quiet for a minute then Colin asked, "Remember when you listed all the contents you could remember that was in your dresser drawer?"

"Yes," Darcy replied.

Colin put down his mug and pulled out his notebook. "You said there was an old map. Do you think that map would say where the gold was?"

Darcy ran a hand through her hair. "I don't know Colin, maybe."

"Do you mind if I take a look?"

Darcy shook her head no and Colin stood up and walked back towards her room. She sat there thinking about all the lost years she and her mother could have had here in this cabin.

Colin walked back to the couch where Darcy still sat. "I didn't find a map. Are you absolutely sure it was in the drawer?"

She looked up at Colin, annoyed. "Yes, I'm absolutely sure. I would like to remind you that we came here looking for someone who kidnapped my daughter, remember?"

Colin took a deep breath to calm himself down and not spew something that was going to turn into a full-blown argument. "I know that, Darcy. I'm not worried about the gold. What I am worried about is motive. Did Tommy know about this?"

Darcy stood up and started pacing. "I don't know. It's not exactly like he's a stellar member of the community and I can trust what he says."

"Okay then, let's lock up and go home. Maybe Jack will have some answers. He and your grandfather were best friends, remember? When you're in a war situation you tend to tell your buddies things that you would otherwise keep to yourself."

Darcy stood up and looked around the cabin one last time to make sure everything was locked up. "It's worth a try," Darcy said as she followed Colin out the door.

Chapter 24

When Darcy and Colin pulled up in front of the house, they saw that all the lights in the house were on. Emma was the first one out the door. She hugged her mom then she clung to Colin and started crying harder. Darcy immediately thought of Jack.

"Hey," Colin said, trying to console Emma. "What's wrong?"

Emma wiped her tears away and shook her head. "It's Rebel."

Colin's heart sank, but he wasn't surprised, and Darcy's eyes started to well up as Jack walked out onto the porch.

"What's all this ruckus?" Jack asked gruffly.

Colin looked up at Jack but had difficulty saying the words. "Rebel? He is—" he couldn't finish.

Jack looked at all three of them, flabbergasted. "Rebel's going to be fine. He needs to take it easy and he has a few stitches where the bullet went in, but it missed all his vital organs. He just needs lots of TLC."

Darcy let out a sigh of relief as Emma tried to catch her breath. "I'm sorry, I didn't mean to scare everyone but when I saw you everything came rushing back."

Darcy hugged her tight and kissed the top of her head. "Everything will be okay. Tommy's not going to hurt you, and neither is the other guy. All you need to worry about is spending lots of time with Rebel and helping him to heal. Can you do that?"

Emma wiped away her tears and nodded. She turned and walked back into the house towards where Rebel lay. Darcy sat down in one of the rockers as Jack and Colin took the other chairs sitting on the porch.

"Did you find him?" Jack asked.

Colin looked at him and said, "Not yet, but I think he's hiding out on Darcy's land."

Jack looked out towards the mountains. "That's a lot of land to cover. It's gonna be hard to find him in that dense forest."

Colin looked at Darcy. "We're hoping maybe you can help us out."

Jack took a deep breath. "Well, I'm not a young guy any more, but I'd be willing to walk the forest with you."

Colin shook his head. "Not that kind of help. While we were at the cabin Darcy found this letter." He handed it to Jack. When Jack finished, he sighed, but didn't say anything. Colin continued. "There was also an old map that Darcy said is now missing. We were hoping that maybe you would know something about that."

Jack stood up and winced when he tried to move his arm. "Last I knew, you were looking for the person that took Emma. I may not be the smartest man in the world, but searching for gold is not something I'm interested in looking for." He opened the door to let himself into the house, but Darcy stopped him.

"I don't care about the gold, Jack, but we think it's all connected. If you know anything at all, please help us. I won't sleep at night knowing that Emma might still be in danger."

Jack sighed and said, "Actually, I do know a little something about this. It's a long story, and I swore I'd never tell anyone but after what's happened, I think your grandpa will be okay if I broke my promise." Jack sat back down. "Well, to start with, your cabin has been in your family for generations. As kids, your grandpa and Tommy's daddy, Beauford, were best friends. One day they were running through the woods, as boys will do, and they came across a cave. They dared each other to go into the cave, but both chickened out. The next day they took a flashlight and headed back out to the cave. They saw gold flecks in the stone and figured they were rich. They had it tested to make sure it wasn't fool's gold and to their delight, they were indeed rich. That night they made a pact that no one would know about the gold except the two of them and it stayed that way for many years. Hank and Beauford were best men in each other's weddings and eventually they became family men with wives and kids of their own."

"Then one day Beauford got fired from his job and his family started struggling financially. The two men agreed to take some of the gold and cash it in at a neighboring town, so no one would get suspicious. It kept ol' Beauford afloat for a while, but his wife kept asking where the money came from. The two would argue and Beauford would escape to the bar and start drinking. He was a mean drunk, so it wasn't surprising when he started abusing his wife and Tommy. As time went by, Beauford got greedy and wanted to start mining the mountain as a business and cash in, but your Grandpa Hank had other ideas. Then one night, Beauford was drinking at the bar and spouting off at the mouth. Your Grandpa Hank happened to walk in about the same time that the bartender kicked Beauford out. The two men started shouting at each other out in the street, then came the pushing and shoving, and then Beauford threw the first punch."

Jack looked Darcy in the eye. "But Hank finished the fight. Like I told you before, Darcy, Hank was a great guy, but you didn't want to get on the wrong side of him. Anyways, about that time the draft for the Vietnam War started, and Hank and I were bussed off to war. Beauford stayed behind on account of a bum leg."

Darcy interrupted him. "Did my grandmother know about the gold?"

Jack shook his head. "No, I don't think so. He didn't want her worrying about such things and he knew no one in town believed Beauford. Tommy's mama gained an inheritance and Beauford packed them up and they moved away. Beauford was always about the money." Jack looked out over the mountains. "Finally, Hank and I came back home. The war had been bad and it took its toll on both of us." Jack looked at Colin. "You know that better than anyone, but that's a story for another day."

Colin shook his head. "It's all in the past, Dad. I forgive you."

Jack wiped a tear from his eye and took a shaky breath. "Eventually, Beauford moved back to town. Tommy and your momma started dating and Hank had a bad feeling that Tommy was up to no good. He tried to convince Kim to stop dating him, but she was a stubborn one." Jack smiled ruefully. "Just like you, Darcy."

Darcy smiled back and her heart swelled with pride that she carried on that particular family trait.

Jack cleared his throat and continued. "Unbeknownst to us, Tommy had also heard Beauford's stories of gold and when he was old enough, Beauford took him to the cave and showed him. He swore Tommy to secrecy, but told him that if he married Kim, one day he'd be a rich man."

Colin's phone rang. "Hello?"

"Hey, Sheriff, I ran the name Jason Rutledge through the system and have some information for you. Seems our guy and Tommy were both incarcerated in the Montana State Prison and were cell mates."

Colin looked over at Darcy. "Well, at least we know how they are connected. Thanks!" Colin hung up and said, "Darcy, I think it's time to pay dear old dad a visit. Are you up for that?"

Darcy stood up and looked at Jack. "Can we finish this another time?"

Jack nodded at Darcy and looked quizzically at Colin.

Darcy interrupted Jack's thoughts by asking. "Do you mind if Emma stays with you?"

Jack laughed. "I think you should probably ask Emma if she minds staying here with me. She's being a mother hen and sometimes I'm not as patient as I should be."

Darcy leaned down and kissed Jack's cheek. She looked at Colin. "Let's go."

They drove in silence, each processing what Jack had told them and then Colin asked, "Darcy, how are you at acting?"

Darcy looked at him, confused, and said, "I can hold my own, why?"

Colin smiled. "I just came up with an idea of how Tommy is going to lead us straight to Jason."

The two walked into the state penitentiary and sat at a table, waiting for the guards to bring Tommy in. He had a sling on his right arm where Darcy had shot him. She couldn't help but smile at the thought of his misery.

Tommy glared at the two of them. "What do you want? I already told my lawyer and the cops everything I know."

He looked at Darcy and smiled. "Guess you were surprised to learn I wasn't the only one involved in this mess. Your precious 'Adam' was in as deep as I was."

Darcy clenched her hands under the table to keep from reaching over and smacking Tommy in the head.

Colin took her hand in his to remind her to stay in control. He leaned back, looking relaxed and said, "Seems your story about having a partner named Jason Rutledge working with you didn't pan out. He had a rock-hard alibi." Colin let go of Darcy's hand and leaned over the table menacingly. "So once again, Tommy, is there anything you want to tell us?"

Tommy stood up, outraged, as the guards started walking toward him. He saw them and calmed down. "He's lying. I had nothing to do with kidnapping that girl."

Darcy couldn't hold back any more. "That girl has a name and it's Emma. She's your granddaughter, for God's sake and I'm going to make damned sure you never get to set eyes on her again."

Colin interjected calmly and said, "I talked to Emma and she said that she only remembers you."

Tommy slammed his hand on the table. "She's lying!"

Darcy leaned across the table and said in a threatening tone, "Don't ever call my daughter a liar. The only liar here is you. Maybe if you hadn't traumatized her by taking her hostage, you wouldn't be the only person she sees night after night in her nightmares."

All three sat quiet for a minute and then Colin looked at Darcy. "I guess we'd best get back to the cabin and meet with Jason."

Tommy squinted his eyes. "What are you talking about? What has he told you?"

Darcy stood up and smiled sweetly at Tommy. "Well, seems your friend felt badly about what you had done. He met me at the diner the other day and explained to me that he had legally changed his name to Adam after he got out of prison and that he really did work for Weston Enterprises. He said something about you wanting to get a hold of the land because according to him the hills are full of gold. Naturally, I didn't believe him but then he gave me the map."

Tommy looked livid. "Well, I guess now you know. You're probably going to be foolish just like your grandfather and keep the land."

Darcy laughed and kissed Colin full on the lips. "Oh no, dear Daddy. We're going to mine it and have the biggest wedding this town has ever seen. Of course, Jack will walk me down the aisle since he's the closest thing I have to a father. Emma will be set for life and can choose any college she wants to when she gets older. I also felt bad for what you put Adam through, trying to ruin his reputation after he was trying to make a life for himself, so I told him he will receive ten percent of the earnings." Darcy stood up and continued,

"So after all this I guess some good did come out of it. Too bad you didn't trust me from the beginning."

Tommy held his head in his hands and was speechless. Colin and Darcy stood up to leave then stopped as Colin turned around. "By the way, Tommy, since your information didn't pan out, I stopped by the district attorney's office and told them to continue to charge you with kidnapping." Colin looked at Darcy and smiled. "Are you ready, honey?"

Darcy didn't even look in the direction of Tommy. "Yes, darling, it's a relief to know I will never have to come back here again."

Tommy jumped up. "Wait! I have information about the cave!"

Colin laughed and said, "You don't honestly expect us to believe that do you?"

The door unlatched and slid open as Tommy watched Darcy and Colin walk away.

Once they got in the car, Darcy looked over at Colin. "Do you think it worked?"

Colin slipped on his sunglasses and started up the car. "Oh yeah, if there's one thing I know, it's that people like Tommy only think of self-preservation. They don't care about anything else. By the end of the day, we'll be hearing from him, don't you worry."

Darcy finished making dinner as Jack set the table the best he could. Emma and Colin came in from the barn after taking care of the horses. Darcy looked their way and smiled. She loved seeing how happy Emma looked. She hadn't seen her smile so much since before her dad passed away. "Okay, you two," Darcy ordered. "Get cleaned up, dinner is almost ready." The two shuffled down to the mud room where there was a large sink placed there for just the occasion.

They had just sat down to dinner when Colin's phone rang.

"Aren't you going to answer it?" Darcy asked, hoping it was Tommy.

Colin didn't even look to see who it was. "No, ma'am, it's supper time. We don't take phone calls during dinner. except if it's from the precinct, which this one isn't. Come on now, let's eat."

Darcy looked at him incredulously. "What if it's Tommy?"

Colin looked around the table. "He can wait. It ain't like he's going anywhere."

"Not," Emma corrected. "It's not like he's going anywhere."

Colin looked at her confused and said, "That's what I said."

Emma shook her head and looked conspiratorially at her mother.

Jack laughed. "Son, you've got a lot to learn about living with women." They all laughed as they started eating.

Once dinner was over Darcy couldn't stand it any longer. "Colin, could you please check your phone?"

He pulled out his phone and checked. He smiled. "What did I tell you? Tommy is ready to talk. We'll swing over there in the morning."

"What?" Darcy asked shocked. "Why not go now? I can't sleep knowing Jason's running loose." She grabbed her jacket and started zipping it up.

Colin huffed, "Damn it, Darcy, just let me do my job for a change. If we go there now, we're giving him the upper hand. If we wait it gives him more time to think about how much he's willing to tell us and how much he's got to lose. Trust me on this."

Darcy groaned and gave in, but she wasn't letting him off the hook that easy. "You'd better be right, Sheriff, because if not, I'll get Tommy to talk, one way or another, and I don't think you'd like it much."

Colin smiled. "I believe you, now let's go out and sit around the fire that Jack and Emma started. It's a beautiful night.

He held out a hand for Darcy as she placed hers in his. They walked out and sat down next to Jack and Emma. They spent the night telling stories, some true and some not so true. They laughed and joked and for the first time in a very long time, Colin discovered what it felt like to be a family. He could see himself spending his life with Darcy and raising Emma. He could also see Jack playing a much bigger part in his life. He felt happy and content. He felt at peace.

Chapter 25

The next morning Darcy and Colin sat across from each other sipping their coffee. "Okay," said Colin. "Please let me do the talking. I promise we will get to the end of this." Darcy opened her mouth to disagree but changed her mind and conceded. This was not a normal feeling for her. They both walked out to his jeep and climbed in. They rode in silence on the way to the prison, each lost in their own thoughts.

They walked into the prison and were taken to the same room they were in the last time. This time Darcy braced herself and took a deep breath, praying that Colin was right and hoping that she wouldn't lose her temper. Tommy walked in. He looked tired, he had spotty facial hair growing, his head had been shaved, and he had a black eye.

Colin shook his head. "Having a little trouble making friends, Tommy?"

Tommy glared at Colin. "They didn't take too kindly to the idea that I kidnapped a child. Which you and I both know is a lie."

Colin leaned back in his seat and crossed his arms in front of his chest. "In my profession it's hard to believe a hardened felon, but that's neither here nor there. Tommy, you're wasting my time, and Darcy and I have a meeting with a developer in a few hours. You called me, so what is it you have to say?"

Tommy looked at the guard and said, "Can you please bring in my lawyer?" The guard nodded and a small wiry public defender with round glasses holding a brown briefcase entered the room.

He opened the briefcase and pulled out a pile of papers, then cleared his throat. "My client would like to plead to accessory to kidnapping in exchange for your re-examination of Jason Rutledge."

Colin shook his head and smiled at Tommy. "Sorry, that is something I will make sure that the DA won't concede on. Is that all you've got, Tommy?"

Tommy tried to contain his temper and said, "Please let my lawyer finish what he was saying." Colin kept his eyes on Tommy as the lawyer continued. "Tommy also has information to the whereabouts of the cave that you are looking for."

Darcy exchanged a glance with Colin. She strongly suspected that was where Jason was hiding out. She opened her mouth to speak but Colin spoke first. "Well, that's mighty generous of you, Tommy, but the fact is we have a map to the cave remember?"

Tommy smiled. "Oh yeah, I remember." He leaned forward, smiling. "And I also know that you're bluffing. There isn't a map leading to the cave. There never was. I know where that cave is. My daddy made sure of that.

I can lead you there, then you can see for yourself that I'm not lying."

Darcy interjected. "Why do you care what we think?"

Tommy shrugged. "I don't, but I want to prove that Jason is lying and if he ain't turned up yet then chances are he found that cave and he is hiding out in it. I'll be damned if I'm going to pay for his crimes. If these guys think I kidnapped the kid, I'm going to have more than just a black eye."

Colin looked at Darcy and then said, "Darcy, it's your call. I don't care either way. We can leave now and go on with our lives or we can let Tommy con us again." Tommy slammed his fist on the table. "Sheriff, I swear I did not kidnap that kid." Darcy stood up and glared at Tommy, "That kid is your granddaughter. That kid has a name. That kid has had nightmares every night because of you." Tommy sat back defeated. "Darcy, I'm begging you. Please, please believe me. I'm not lying. I know you don't have to believe me but let me make it up to you. Don't you want to know for sure if I'm lying or not? Will you be able to sleep at night wondering if Jason, who is still out there, was the one who kidnapped Emma?"

Darcy shrugged and looked at her watch, "I don't have to worry about Jason. All I have to worry about is having you behind bars far away from me and my daughter." All three sat in silence. Tommy watched her pleadingly. Darcy looked at Colin then sighed dramatically. "Fine. Write down how to get to the cave and we'll let you know what we find out." She dug into her purse looking for a pen and paper.

Tommy shook his head. "I can't. I have to show you. You can't get there by car or even by an off-road vehicle. It'll take days to walk it and even then, I'm not sure I can get you to the right place. My daddy had a horse, it's over on Grimley's farm. That horse knows the way. I can lead you there."

Colin looked at Tommy and shook his head. "Now you know we can't do that."

Tommy said earnestly, "Please, Sheriff. They're going to kill me in here if I don't find Jason."

Colin thought for a moment. "I'll see what I can do. Until then I'll have them lock you up in solitary."

Colin dropped Darcy off at the ranch, checked on Jack and Rebel, and then left to go back to the precinct. As he was driving, he changed his mind and made a quick right towards Grimley's farm. He pulled onto the dirt driveway leading up to the house and saw that Old Man Grimley was out saddling up one of his horses. "Hey there, Matt," Colin said reaching out and running his hand along the horse's mane. "I see you're heading out, but I'm hoping that maybe you can spare a few minutes to answer a few questions?"

Matt tipped his cowboy hat back and looked at Colin. "Wish I could, Sheriff, but I've got some cattle getting loose through a break in the fence. I've got to get out there before I lose my livestock."

Colin shook his head in sympathy, he remembered those days on the ranch with his own grandfather. "Well, Matt, if you'd like a hand, I'd be happy to help you out and then we can talk."

Matt smiled. "I never turn down good help. Are you sure you remember how to mend a fence, Sheriff? Your hands might get a little dirty." The men had known each other for years and had always been friends.

Colin laughed. "I grew up mending fences, remember??"

Matt laughed. "Yeah, I remember, then you became sheriff and got all soft."

Colin held onto the mare while Matt walked into the stables and walked out with a beautiful pinto. She held her head high as she pranced out alongside Matt. Her brown and white colors ebbed and flowed like the tide. Matt walked her over to Colin then mounted his own horse. "That one's Queenie and she's pretty tame. You shouldn't have any trouble with her. Saddle her up and let's get going."

Colin shook his head and smiled. "It won't take me long so don't get too comfortable up there."

The two men rode slowly side by side, checking the fence for the break. Matt broke the silence first. "So, what brings you out my way?"

Colin's face grew serious. "Tommy Blackwell."

Matt whistled. "I haven't heard that name in a long time. Is he back around here?"

"Sort of, he's currently locked up in the Montana State Prison."

"What does that have to do with me?" Matt asked.

"Tommy mentioned that you're keeping one of his daddy's horses here on the farm."

Matt turned towards Colin. "You're right. Once old Beauford passed on and Tommy left town, I took the horse in and have been taking care of it ever since. He's getting on in age, though. What's this all about?"

Colin relayed the information that Tommy had told him about the horse and the cave on Darcy's land. He didn't mention the gold, since that was irrelevant. "Do you think Tommy could be telling the truth? Could that old horse actually lead him to the cave?"

Matt was quiet for a moment then said, "I don't know, but if someone is hiding out in that cave and the only way to get to it is by horseback and you don't know where you're going, then I'd give it a try. I mean, a horse can recognize previous owners from years past, so who knows?"

They rode silently the rest of the way as Colin tried to decide what to do. It was crazy to even consider turning Tommy loose and trusting that he would lead them to Jason, wasn't it? He thought of Emma and knew that he'd do anything to protect her, so maybe taking a chance that Tommy was right wasn't so crazy after all. The two men made quick work of patching the fence, then Colin asked, "Do you mind if I borrow Beauford's horse tomorrow morning? I promise we'll take it easy on her."

Colin spent the rest of the day setting up things for the next day. He decided to take a chance and have Tommy go along but that didn't mean he was going to trust him. He also knew that if the cave did contain gold, the less people who knew about it the better. He checked the closet to make sure that his Kevlar vest was still hanging inside then he called his deputy into his office to go over the plan.

***

The next morning Colin opened his eyes and listened as Darcy puttered around in the kitchen making coffee. He thought about what laid ahead and hoped all would go as planned. With any luck, Jason would be in custody by the end of the day. Colin got dressed and walked out to the kitchen. He took Darcy in his arms and kissed her softly then he reached for the coffee mug sitting on the counter.

Darcy looked at him expectantly. "So, when do we leave?"

Colin nearly spat out his coffee and shook his head. "Oh no, Darcy, definitely not. There is no way you're going along."

Darcy leaned against the counter and crossed her arms which Colin already knew meant he was in for a fight. "We can do this the easy way or the hard way.

Which will it be?" Darcy asked sweetly. "That is my land. He's messing with my life. He hurt my daughter. I will not sit by and do nothing."

Colin stood up and walked towards her. He tilted her face towards his. He could see the stubbornness in her eyes. "I know what's at stake Darcy. I promise you I will bring him in and I will make sure he pays for what he has done to you and to Emma, but I can't be out there doing my job and worrying about you at the same time. It's not safe. Tommy can't be trusted, you know that. I won't put you in harm's way."

Darcy sighed. "Well, I guess you've made up your mind."

Colin sighed in relief. "Thank you for understanding." He finished off his coffee and put on his hat. He kissed her once more and walked outside to hook the horse trailer to his jeep.

Once Colin had left, Darcy woke up Jack. "Okay, Jack, he's gone. We have just enough time to grab your trailer and get our horses to the cabin before they get there."

Jack looked serious. "Are you sure you still want to do this?"

Darcy was already putting on her coat. "Yes, no one messes with my family and gets away with it."

Jack shook his head and mumbled, "Colin isn't gonna be happy about this and for once I agree with him."

Darcy looked at him without backing down. "Jack, you know I'm going to do this, with or without you."

He sighed and looked at the ceiling in defeat. "Oh, don't I know it. Go on and call the neighbor to keep an eye on Emma while I get dressed."

Jack and Darcy were already saddled up and in the woods by the time Colin pulled up. He left Tommy in the car with the deputy while he led the horses out of the trailer and saddled them up. Tommy remained handcuffed as he was taken out of the car. Tommy eyed the horses. "How am I supposed to get on the horse with these handcuffs?"

Colin looked at him and smiled. "You used to be a country boy, Tommy, so surely you can get yourself on a horse, after all, this was your idea."

Tommy looked at his hands. "It'd be a lot easier if these cuffs weren't on my wrist."

"Well, you'd better get used to them because they're staying on," Colin finished putting on his Kevlar vest and then looked at the deputy. "Let's get a move on, we're losing daylight." The three men started towards the woods with Tommy in the lead. It was quiet as they loped along, watching for tree roots or holes that could injure the horses. Darcy and Jack stayed out of sight as they followed a safe distance behind. Darcy tried to inch her way a little closer as a thin branch cracked on the ground underneath her.

Colin stopped and looked in the direction of the sound. He looked at the deputy. "Did you hear that?"

The deputy nodded. "I'll keep an eye on Tommy," he said to Colin. "You go check it out."

Colin pulled out his weapon and started off towards the northeast. It didn't take long to see the body of a horse about twenty feet away, but the person was hidden behind a tree trunk. Colin yelled, "Come out with your hands up!" He waited but there was no response. "I'm only going to say this one last time," Colin shouted. "Come out now or I'll shoot and ask questions later." Darcy gently kicked the mare so that Colin could see her. "Damn it, Darcy, what in the hell are you doing? I could have shot you!"

Darcy looked first at Tommy and then at Colin. She opened her mouth to speak just as Jack brought his horse to stand next to hers.

"Jack?" Colin sputtered. "You're in on this too?"

Jack smiled wryly. "Well, son, she's kind of hard to say no to."

Colin was speechless then Tommy spoke up. "Aww, c'mon, Sheriff, let them tag along, after all this is her land and she has a right to know what's on it."

Darcy looked from Tommy to Colin. "We could debate this all day, but we're going to be losing daylight so if you want to wrap this up, I say we should get going."

Colin was seething but she was right, they were losing daylight, so he turned his horse around and rode along the other side of Tommy. Jack and Darcy followed quietly behind.

Tommy was the first to break the silence. "Going up to that cave full of gold was the only time I remembered spending time with my pa. Any other time he was in the bars drinking. You know a thing or two about that don't you, Colin?"

Colin gritted his teeth and refused to answer. The quicker this was over with the better, as far as he was concerned. Tommy could run off at the mouth all the wanted but he wasn't going to take the bait. His mind was on other things, like Darcy once again disregarding his request and putting herself in the middle of something dangerous.

Darcy on the other hand, did take the bait. "Well, Tommy, consider yourself lucky, I don't have a single memory of my dad. It seems I was the last thing on his mind."

Tommy stopped his horse and looked back at Darcy.

"That's not true."

Colin glared at Tommy. "Keep going."

Tommy started up again then said, "I'm sorry. Is that what you want to hear, Darcy?"

Darcy could feel the rage she had suppressed for so long coming to the top. "Sorry for what, Tommy? Beating my mom? Kidnapping and punching my daughter? Disappearing off the face of the earth?"

Jack interjected, "Darcy, that man ain't worth arguing with. He's been this way ever since I've known him."

Tommy scoffed. "What did I tell you, Darcy? This town won't ever allow me to change. I'll always be known as the bad kid, the one you don't want hanging around. I have never been accepted."

Darcy retorted, "That's where you're wrong. This town didn't make you who you are. You did that all on your own."

Tommy shook his head. "That's where you're wrong, darlin. The beatings my daddy gave me when I didn't bring home enough cash or steal enough valuables or hell, just because he felt like it, that's what made me who I am. A no bit con man without a nickel to his name. I've only done two things right in my life: one was becoming your daddy and the other was leaving so you could have a better life than I did."

Darcy remained quiet as they stopped by a creek so the horses could have a drink and rest. Tommy sat against a tree trunk with his arms resting across his knees, watching Darcy. She looked so much like her mother. After the horses drank, she sat down next to Jack on a flat rock.

Tommy cleared his throat and Colin looked over at him. "You okay Tommy?"

"Yeah, Sheriff, just an old man reminiscing is all."

Jack looked over at him. "We all live with demons, Tommy, it's what you do afterward that matters. Maybe you should spend a little less time reminiscing and a little more time living in the present."

Tommy looked over at Jack. "You may be right, but when you're looking at prison time in the present, then the past doesn't seem so bad. I'll never forget the feeling I got when Darcy's momma agreed to marry me."

Darcy replied sarcastically, "Let me guess, you couldn't believe that you actually struck it rich and to think she actually thought you loved her."

Tommy looked over at her. "I felt rich all right, but not in the way you're thinking. I couldn't believe someone that beautiful, that good, that perfect, saw something in me that I couldn't even see in myself. When we went back to the cabin to tell your grandparents the news, your Grandpa Hank forbid us to marry. When your momma looked at your grandma, she knew they wouldn't change their minds. My daddy, on the other hand, was thrilled and celebrated by drinking even more and rambling on about how Hank was finally getting what he deserved and how him and I were going to strike it rich. Then your momma discovered she was pregnant, and I knew we couldn't stay here. The town already had their opinion of me, her parents weren't gonna let us marry, and my old man was going to get his hands on that gold come hell or high water. So, we left, and we never looked back.

"At first everything was going good and we were happy, but then things just kept getting harder and harder. Your momma never complained, but I knew I was a failure and like my old man, I started drinking and turning mean. It's something I'm ashamed of to this very day and I want you to know, Darcy, that your momma was a good woman, and she deserved a lot better than me. One day I hope you'll understand. I made a lot of mistakes and I ain't making excuses, but I really hope that one day I can make it right by you."

Colin stood up and helped Tommy up. "Let's get going, Tommy. Family bonding time is over."

Darcy mounted her horse and looked away. She didn't want anyone to see the tears quietly trickling down her cheek. She missed her mom and wished she could talk to her to help her understand all the different feelings welling up inside of her.

They rode the rest of the way in silence until they reached the opening of a cave. "Here it is," said Tommy.

Colin looked at Tommy then the deputy. "Keep him here while I go check things out."

"Stop right there, Sheriff," a voice shouted from inside the cave. "You've gone far enough."

Tommy taunted Jason. "You didn't actually think you were going to get away with this did you?"

Jason stepped out where everyone could see him. He was holding the rifle that Darcy had left in her room. Colin calmly said, "Jason, we just want to talk. Put down the rifle."

Jason shook his head. "I ain't going back to prison, Sheriff. I was just paying back a debt to Tommy and I never hurt the girl, I swear it. The whole plan was Tommy's idea."

Colin could hear the panic in Jason's voice and calmly said, "Why don't you put the gun down and me, you, and Tommy will talk about this in a reasonable way. No one has to get hurt. I just want to understand what's going on."

Jason swung the rifle from left to right. "I don't think so. You aren't going to believe me. Why would you?"

Darcy slowly began to dismount from her horse. Jason yelled, "Darcy, I suggest you climb back on that horse and ride away."

Colin's eyes never left Jason's. "I suggest you follow the man's suggestion Darcy." Darcy blew out a breath in exasperation.

Jack spoke up. "Jason, there are four people who are armed and only one of you. Now the way I see it, the odds aren't in your favor. If you cooperate now, maybe the sheriff will be lenient on you."

Jason looked at Colin, who shrugged. "I'm sure we could work something out."

Jason thought for a minute and then yelled, "Jack, you may be right, and I know I'm outnumbered. Sheriff, I appreciate that you'd be willing to work something out, but somehow, I'm pretty sure that whatever you come up with will still involve prison time. The way I see it, I'm still holding the winning hand."

Jason held up a stack of papers and waved them towards Darcy. "Darcy, all you've got to do is sign this deed for the property and I can just be on my way. No harm, no foul. You'll never see me again. You have my word on it."

Darcy scoffed. "You don't expect me to believe that for a minute, do you? There's no way I would ever turn my family's land over to you. As far as I'm concerned you can rot in hell."

Jason laughed and said, "Maybe this will change your mind. Emma, come on out here darlin'."

Darcy felt the ground shift underneath her as she saw her daughter, scratched up, dirty, and crying. She could feel her body getting hot as her rage grew from within her. She was not going to allow these men to hurt her or her daughter ever again. She quietly slid down from her horse while Jason was looking at Colin.

Jack watched her silently, not wanting to give her away, but also ready in case she needed help. Darcy walked closer towards the cave hoping Jason wouldn't spot her. She reached the huge maple tree and hid behind its vast trunk. She knew it was now or never. She stepped out from behind it, hoping to run and push Emma out of the way, but Jason suddenly turned the rifle towards her and yelled, "I suggest you stop right there."

While his attention was on Darcy, Tommy kicked his horse forcing the powerful animal to jump and run straight towards Jason. Jason swung his rifle ready to fire but was too late as the horse knocked him to the ground. Tommy also fell to the ground and felt something break. He was struggling to breathe as he

272

looked around him and saw Jason lying on the ground with blood oozing from his head.

Darcy ran towards Emma and hugged her close, then she ran over to Tommy. "Are you all right?" she asked with a shaky voice.

Tommy looked up at her. "Good as ever. Look, Darcy, I'm sorry for all of this. You and Emma deserved better than me. I swear to you I will never bother you again. I just want you to be happy. I'll spend the rest of my days in jail and I don't ever want you to think about me again. Your momma was right to tell you that I was dead. You're better off that way."

Darcy was crying as she knelt down beside him. "Be that as it may, you also saved Emma and for that I will always be eternally grateful."

Colin walked over towards Tommy. "Darcy, please move away. He's a criminal in the state's possession and I'm not going to take a chance of putting you or Emma in harm's way ever again."

Darcy looked up in surprise and said, "He may be a criminal, but he helped to save Emma, and me for that matter, and it doesn't take a rocket scientist to see that he's obviously hurt. I'm sure I'm safe and if not, I can still take care of myself."

Tommy chuckled and said, "Yep, you're just like your momma, and I say that in the highest esteem. I'm proud of you, Darcy, and I'm so thankful that you didn't turn out like me."

Colin looked down at him and placed his arm possessively around Darcy. "I'm glad she didn't turn out like you either, Tommy." Darcy glared at him and then he cleared his throat. "What you did here was stupid and dangerous. You could have gotten someone killed, but the fact is you didn't, not even Jason over there." Colin nodded his head in Jason's direction and heard a groan as the man was coming to. "But you look like you're hurt and in need of medical attention, so we'd best get going before the sun goes down."

"Wait a minute," Emma shouted incredulously. "Are you saying that he really is my grandpa?" Darcy nodded her head confirming Emma's statement. "Why am I always the last to know these things?" Emma said, pouting.

Darcy put her arm around her daughter and kissed her on top of the head. "It's a long story and I promise we will tell you everything."

Tommy looked up at her. "We?"

She wiped away a stray tear and smiled. "Yes, Tommy, I said we."

Colin read Jason his rights and helped him up onto one of the horses. His head wound appeared to be superficial and Colin surmised that the total extent of his injuries might be a couple of stitches and perhaps a concussion. The deputy accompanying Jason read him his Miranda rights.

Colin then walked over to Tommy. "Can you get up on your own?" Tommy slowly sat up, grimacing in pain and holding his side. Darcy stood by Tommy's side. "I'll help you up on the horse." Colin interjected. "He'll be riding with me."

Darcy opened her mouth to disagree but knew this was an argument she wasn't going to win. She allowed Tommy to lean against her and he grunted as he pulled himself up and onto the saddle. Colin climbed on behind him and then looked at Darcy. "Emma should ride with you."

Darcy nodded and was going to help Emma up onto the saddle but Emma put out her hand. "I can do this on my own, Mom. Jack's been teaching me to ride."

Darcy looked over at Jack who nodded in agreement. Once Emma was settled, Darcy climbed up behind her.

The trip home seemed quicker than the trip out to the cave. Once they arrived back at the cabin, two ambulances were waiting along with other police officers. Colin filled in his officers and walked over towards the jeep.

"Jack, Emma, Darcy, climb in." Colin yelled, "We're going to the hospital."

Emma was the first to speak. "What for?"

Colin met Darcy's eyes and said, "To check on Tommy. He did save both my girls' lives and for that the least I can do is make sure he's going to be okay."

Darcy hugged him tight as the tears started to flow once again. Much to Emma's delight, Colin turned on the siren as they sped through town.

Once at the hospital, Darcy ran up to the desk to ask about Tommy. The doctor walked out into lobby and greeted them. He shook Colin's hand and Colin introduced Darcy and Emma.

"Is he going to be, okay?" Darcy asked.

The doctor looked at her and then Colin. "He suffered a couple of broken ribs and he has a slight concussion, but he should start feeling better in a couple of days."

Darcy blew out a sigh of relief. "Can we see him?"

The doctor looked at Colin who gave his permission for Darcy and Emma to visit Tommy.

All three of them walked into the hospital room and saw Tommy hooked up to IV tubes and monitors. He looked towards them when the door opened and smiled sadly. "Hi, I figured I'd be under arrest and wouldn't be allowed to see anyone."

Darcy smiled at Tommy through tear filled eyes and said, "I have some pull with the local sheriff in town."

Colin cleared his throat and said, "I'm going to talk to the district attorney about cutting a deal. If you didn't do what you did to Jason, who knows how this would have turned out."

Tommy smiled and said, "That's mighty kind of you, Sheriff, but I have a daughter and a granddaughter to think of. What kind of man would I be if I didn't lead by example? Emma here needs to know that there are consequences for my actions. I did something wrong and the only way to make it right is to do my time."

Colin looked at him, clearly confused. "Are you saying you are willing to go to prison and pay for your crimes? You don't want to work out a deal?"

Tommy looked up a Darcy. "That's exactly what I'm saying, Sheriff."

Darcy interjected. "But, Tommy, I just got you back I don't want to lose you again."

Jack was silent as he watched the two men interacting. He thought of his own mistakes and knew that being separated wasn't going to help Tommy nor Darcy and Emma. "If I can interrupt here for a minute, Colin, I'd like to propose another idea."

Colin looked at Jack, clearly confused, and Tommy eyed him with interest.

"What is it, Jack?" Emma asked.

Jack walked closer and said, "Well, it's a bit of a compromise." He looked at Tommy and then at Colin. "What if we struck a deal where Tommy can remain in town at the local jail instead of going to prison? That way if Darcy wants to work things out with Tommy, she can, and Tommy can still be held accountable for his actions when he goes to trial."

Colin looked at Tommy. "Well, what do you say?"

Tommy was quiet then said, "I'll leave this up to the girls. I've made a lot of mistakes and I have no right to ask for forgiveness."

Jack could feel himself choke up and he took a deep breath.

Tommy looked at everyone standing in his room, then his eyes came to rest on Darcy. He spoke gruffly. "You've got a great family there, but given the chance, I'd like to become part of it."

Darcy watched her daughter walk closer to Tommy. "Well, if you're my grandpa then I expect you to be around. Can you do that?"

Tommy's eyes started filling with tears. He tried to clear his throat and said huskily, "I'd love to do that."

Colin walked closer to Darcy and kissed her forehead. "Well now that it's settled," Colin said. "I guess I should also tell you, Tommy, that I intend on marrying Darcy if she'd agree to it and if you're all right with it."

Darcy looked up at Colin, her eyes full of all the emotions she had bottled up throughout the years to keep love at bay.

Tommy held out his hand to Colin. "I can't think of anyone better to take care of my two girls."

Emma squealed and clapped her hands before asking, "Are you marrying my mom?"

Colin smiled and pulled his gaze away from Darcy. "Not yet. I have to do something else first."

He walked over to Emma and took both of her hands. "Emma, would it be okay if I married your mom and we became a family?"

Emma was speechless and her eyes welled up. She knew she'd always have a place in her heart for her dad, but somehow Colin had also taken up residence there. She took a shaky breath. "I would love that but—"

Colin looked at her in surprise. "But what, sweetheart?"

Emma looked from Colin to Darcy, then back to Colin. "But you should know my mom can be a bit of a handful and at times very stubborn."

Darcy opened her mouth to disagree, but Emma stopped her before she had a chance to reply. Her daughter, who made it a mission to keep people at arm's length, who had difficulty trusting others, was wrapping her arms around Colin and smiling.

Jack looked at his son. "Well, you can't just blurt out asking a woman to marry you without a ring."

Colin looked around and groaned. "I completely forgot about the ring."

Jack reached into his back pocket and pulled out his wallet. He sifted through a few dollar bills and some business cards then pulled out a wedding ring. "This was your momma's. She threw it at me when she told me to leave. I think she'd approve of you giving it to Darcy."

Colin walked towards his father and gently took the ring from him. Both men had tears in their eyes. Colin hugged his dad and walked towards Darcy. He bent down on one knee and looked up at Darcy. He cleared his throat. "Darcy, will you do me the honor of being my wife?"

Darcy was speechless as she looked at the small, beautiful ring that Colin was holding in front of her. She looked at Tommy then Emma and then Jack, her family.

Colin couldn't stand the silence any longer. "Well?"

She took a big breath and smiled. "Yes, yes I will marry you."

Colin stood up and took Darcy in his arms. "I love you," he whispered right before he kissed her.

"I love you too."

Chapter 26

Darcy heard a squeal from her daughter and then laughter. She stood up from her work on the computer, stretched her back, and walked over to the window. She pushed the curtain back to see Emma standing beside the lake with a stick in her hand and Rebel impatiently waiting for her to throw it. The stick flew through the air and barely landed in the water before Rebel jumped in to retrieve it, causing an influx of water, drenching Emma again. There was another squeal as Rebel proudly carried the stick back out of the lake. Darcy smiled and watched the interaction between the two. She still couldn't believe how much had changed in the span of a year and a half.

Colin walked up behind her and kissed her on the neck as he wrapped his arms around Darcy's swollen belly. "How's our newest addition coming along?"

She smiled and turned to wrap her arms around his neck. "She's coming along perfectly." Darcy pulled away and looked at him as she reached for a chocolate bar, one of her many cravings. She took a bite then said, "I was just thinking about how much has changed since we've met and gotten married."

Colin laughed huskily as he reached over and took a bite of her chocolate bar. "It's been quite a year, but one I wouldn't change for the world." He leaned over to kiss her again.

Emma stepped into the cabin soaking wet. "What happened?" Darcy asked as she reached for a kitchen towel and tossed it to Emma.

Emma groaned. "Rebel thought it would be more fun pushing me into the lake instead of chasing a stick." Rebel looked up at Emma and gave a small wag of his tail and his soulful eyes begging for forgiveness.

Colin laughed and said, "Well, I'll drive you home so you can get changed. We have to be at the jail by four o'clock if we're going to visit Tommy."

Emma smiled. "Is Jack coming too?"

Colin shook his head. "No, he's almost finished putting on his addition to the house."

Emma crossed her arms and tried to look angry. "How come I'm the last to know this? I thought he was building a nursery for the baby."

Colin looked at his wife then back to Emma. "With two daughters and your mom, I think I'm going to need some male reinforcement." Emma pretended to look offended as Colin and Darcy laughed.

Colin walked over and kissed Darcy on the cheek. "We'll be back to pick you up in a couple of hours so be ready, okay?"

Darcy smiled. "I will. Now you two get going so I can get some work done in my new office." Emma and

Colin left in the jeep as Darcy looked around the little cabin. She loved it here and she couldn't think of a better place to write. She picked up her laptop and opened up to a blank page. Her heart swelled with pride at the thought of writing her first book. She typed the title in the center of the paper, <u>Dark Secrets</u>, and then began to write.

Made in the USA
Middletown, DE
25 February 2022

61807077R00168